DANNY AND LIFE ON BLUFF POINT

MY HORSE SALLY

DATE DUE

DISCARD

Penn Yan

Keuka
Park

Branchport

home of
Little
Bird

Bluff
Point

our
House

Keuka
Lake

DANNY AND LIFE ON BLUFF POINT

My Horse Sally

Mary Ellen Lee

iUniverse, Inc.
New York Lincoln Shanghai

DANNY AND LIFE ON BLUFF POINT
My Horse Sally

iUniverse books may be ordered through booksellers or by contacting:

iUniverse
2021 Pine Lake Road, Suite 100
Lincoln, NE 68512
www.iuniverse.com
1-800-Authors (1-800-288-4677)

ISBN-13: 978-0-595-36084-0 (pbk)
ISBN-13: 978-0-595-80532-7 (ebk)
ISBN-10: 0-595-36084-X (pbk)
ISBN-10: 0-595-80532-9 (ebk)

Printed in the United States of America

This work is dedicated to my parents who often reminded me happiness is a choice.

Contents

▼

ACKNOWLEDGMENTS

My thanks go to John Creamer and Joanie Hand, Reference Librarian and Local History Librarian respectively, of the Penn Yan Public Library. I also wish to thank Frances Dumas, Yates County Historian for her thoughtful help regarding the Seneca Indians in Yates County.

My special thanks go to Judi Gibbs, classmate and best friend, for her help with the history of the First Baptist Church of Penn Yan.

CHAPTER 1

▼

HIDE AND SEEK

"It's just not fair," wails little Carolyn. She stomps her foot on the bare wood floor. "Danny always hides someplace where I can't find him."

I must not laugh as my littlest sister is standing only a few feet away from me. I am sitting on the floor under the big dining room table, right in the center. My knees are drawn up to make me as small as possible. She will not see me unless she gets down on her hands and knees to look under the table.

Breathing quietly is hard but I am trying. I can hear sister Mary quickly walking toward the dining room from the family parlor. She had been looking for me behind the big horsehair sofa. It is Saturday forenoon and we are playing hide-and-seek in the house as it is raining and cold. Rain is common during April in upstate New York. This year, 1895, is particularly wet and with the rain comes the mud.

Carolyn is five years old and is looking forward to going to school with us come September. My littlest sister has light yellow brown hair and bright blue eyes. She is wearing her cloud dress that is a hand-me-down from Mary. Her favorite things to do are play with our cat, Clara and help Mary set the table for dinner.

"I'm sure he isn't in the parlor," Mary states. "And he said he wouldn't hide in the attic or cellar so where can he be? We have looked everywhere." Mary is eight and has the same eye and hair color as Carolyn. Our Pa calls her Missy sometimes. Mary doesn't seem afraid of anything.

The chairs are all pushed in under the table making a nice little hiding spot. The table cloth drapes down too. It is a good place of concealment.

Suddenly there is a funny sound behind me. I carefully turn my head to look. There is Clara our house cat walking under the table toward me. She is making one of her greeting sounds. Bruuummm, brummmrow.

Clara is a gray tiger. Her job is to keep the house free of mice and rats. She does a very good job doing this as she is a great hunter. Clara caught a mouse the other day and boxed the half dead animal with both paws. Ma put her out in the woodshed while she ate her treasure.

Clara is also purring loudly. She is going to give away my hiding place. The girls are sure to have seen and heard her. She sits by my side but is still making her cat talk sounds. I give here a little hug and rub her head to make her be quiet. She purrs even more loudly.

"Here Clara," Carolyn calls. The table cloth moves. "I found you, I found you, Danny," she exclaims.

"You wouldn't have found me so quickly if Clara hadn't walked under the table," I say as I crawl out.

"Good job," Mary says to Carolyn. "Now it's our turn to hide and there are no places off limits. Start counting, Danny."

"Does that mean you might hide in the attic or basement?" Carolyn asks. A worried look is on her face.

"Yes it does," Mary says proudly. She isn't afraid of the dark as I am.

"But I don't want to hide in the attic or basement."

"Well, you don't have to," I say. "Hide wherever you wish." I hope Mary doesn't hide in the attic as I dislike going up there. It gives me the creeping willies. It is dark and the walls are made of bare lath and plaster. The lath look like the ribs of a skeleton. I try my best not to be afraid of the dark. I don't always succeed.

I am ten years old and like to daydream and tell myself stories. This sometimes gets me into trouble. I have dark hair and blue eyes like my

Pa. I'm also teaching myself to sketch. It is sure difficult to put on paper what I see but I think I'm getting better at it.

"Oh." A bright look comes on her face. She has thought of a spot.

I close my eyes and begin to slowly count to ten. "One, two, three." I can hear the scurrying of little feet and hushed giggles. "Four, five, six." More giggles then silence. "Seven, eight, nine, ten. Here I come, ready or not."

The first place I look is under the table as sometimes Carolyn hides in the place last found. She isn't there. I look down the basement stairs. Too dark. Even Mary wouldn't go down there without a light. I hope she isn't down there as I don't want to go down into the basement to look for her. I hate dark places. She doesn't seem to mind if there is some light.

I find Carolyn under her bed in the girls' bedroom. Together we look for Mary. She is not in the wardrobes in the bedrooms, nor under the beds. She must be up in the attic. There are not many places to hide in the house. This game is better played out of doors where there are lots of places to hide.

As I open the door that leads to the attic stairs Carolyn says, "I don't want to go up there."

"That's all right. I'll look for her. You can stay here."

Boldly I run up the dark stairway. There is some light up here from the small ventilation openings under the eaves. They don't help much on such a dark, rainy day. I can hear the rain pattering on the roof and feel the cold damp air.

Right in the center of the attic is a large pile of dusty old trunks and wooden boxes. Some of the trunks are the old round top kind. Mary must be behind them. She isn't. I check through the other stuff piled on the rough planks that make up the attic floor. I carefully look all around in the dim light, no Mary.

The chimney. I haven't looked behind it. I don't want to go there as it is in a particularly dark spot. Its rough mortar has many dusty spider webs on it. Ugh! I quickly look behind the chimney. Still, no little sister. She is just not in the attic.

Some of the things that are up here had been left behind by the previous owners of the house. The Jasper Traver family had built the house around 1820. Several families had lived in the house before my grandfather, Daniel Stevens Lee, bought the property in 1884.

The attic is spooky and I want to leave but I look once more around the trunks and boxes. My favorite is the big square trunk. It is made of wood and has brass hinges and corners. It must have been used to carry something very valuable. I wonder who the trunks belonged to. Could they be so old they belonged to Mr. Traver and his wife Fannie? A cold shiver runs down my back. A few belong to my family but the rest are a dusty, spider web-covered mystery. I rush down the dark stairs.

"She isn't up there," I say to Carolyn after I carefully shut the heavy door to the attic.

"Where should we look? Could she be in the woodshed?" Carolyn asks. She has a puzzled look on her chubby pink face.

"Good idea, lets go see," I say. We dash down the back stairs to the kitchen. Mary's coat is hanging on its hook. She wouldn't go in the woodshed without it. It is too cold for that.

"Children, please don't run off anywhere, dinner is almost ready," Ma says as she looks up from her potato mashing.

Ma always seems to be in the kitchen preparing something good for us to eat. She is dressed in her usual brown wool dress and white apron. Her brown hair is pinned to the back of her head with ivory hairpins. Her eyes are hazel and she has a short, small body. I guess that is where I get my small body from. She tells us children we must make the best of what has been given to us. I want to be big and tall like Pa.

"Where is Mary?" Ruthie asks sharply. She and Miss Spaulding have been helping Ma with our dinner. "I have started setting the table that is Mary's job. You two finish," demands our big sister.

"I'll finish the table, Danny. You find Mary," Carolyn offers helpfully.

Today is Miss Spaulding's last day with us. She is our teacher and has been living with us since January. Teacher has been packing her belongings and will move to the home of the Marshall family for the rest of the school term. The school year will end the second week of June as we lost almost a full week of school during the blizzard in January and must make up the time.

"Where is Mary?" Ruthie repeats impatiently. Ruthie is our older sister and is always telling us what to do. She is thirteen and thinks she knows everything about everything. She will be moving to town in September to go to high school. Even if she is bossy, we will miss her. She looks much like our Ma.

All eyes are on me. "I don't know. We were playing hide and seek and haven't been able to find her."

"Mmmaarryy!" Ruthie shouts.

"Ruth, I don't think that was necessary," Ma says from the kitchen. "Take a lamp down in the cellar. Danny, please go upstairs and call for her up there. Please look for her on this floor, Carolyn."

We do as we are told and there still is no sign of Mary. I again open the attic door and climb the steep stairs. This time I have a lamp. On the way up the stairs, I realize there are two different sets of foot prints in the dust going up and only one going down. The set going down must be mine. Mary is in the attic.

"Mary, are you up here?" I shout. I hear muffled sounds coming from our pile of trunks and crates. "Mary, where are you?" More muffled sounds.

Within the lamp light, I can see the dust has been disturbed on the top trunk. There are little fingerprints there. I work the stiff latch and slowly open the lid. There is a tearful Mary wrapped in some old clothes to keep warm.

"Oh, thank you, Danny. I knew you would find me." She stands up in the trunk and gives me a big hug.

"What happened?" I ask.

"I went into the trunk meaning to leave the lid open just a crack but it slipped shut and the latch closed. Golly, I was scared."

"Well, come on, everyone is looking for you and dinner is ready. I hope you learned your lesson about going into a trunk with a latch on it. You know you could have suffocated in there."

"Yes, I understand but how was I to know the lid would slip shut?"

"Lids on trunks have a way of doing that, you should be more careful," sounding like a big brother, I hope.

"That is the last time I will ever hide in a trunk. You can be sure of that." We rush down stairs to the kitchen. Mary helps Carolyn finish setting the dining table.

Ma has prepared a special diner of roast beef, mashed potatoes, gravy, rolls, and preserved peas from our garden. Chocolate cake with walnut frosting is for desert. The smell of baking cake and the roasting beef had made me hungry all day.

The oil lamp over the dining table is casting its warm glow. It is a beautiful sight on such a dark day.

I feel terrible when we have roast beef for I know the meat came from our beef cow that we raised since it was young. Pa and Doc butchered it during the first part of the winter. Doc has been our hired hand for a very long time. He had been hired by Grandpa Lee in 1885 and has been with the family ever since.

I am sad about the butchering of our pigs and of course for our chickens and turkeys. Somehow it doesn't bother me as much about the pigs and poultry though. I guess this is because we don't know them as long as we do a beef cow.

We children have strict instruction to not take the death of an animal personally. But sometimes it is very hard not to. The animals are our friends but farm animals are slaughtered, die or are sold, it is a common event, part of farm life.

We don't have any beef cows now. Pa has talked of getting a bull and selling his services. Our Pa would then raise a few beef cows to sell and for our family use. This would be a new business for him and perhaps new responsibilities for me.

Today is our last dinner with Miss Spaulding. She will leave our house tomorrow morning. Of course we will see her at school, but it won't be the same as having her in the house.

When she first came early in January, I thought it would be awful having her with us. Now I know I made a mistake assuming the worst. I know now it is much better to wait awhile before drawing conclusions about a situation. Then you have something on which to base your judgment. It is a sad day because Miss Spaulding is our friend as well as our teacher.

The men come striding into the kitchen. They have left their boots and coveralls in the woodshed as they are very dirty.

"It has mostly stopped raining, Danny," Pa says. "We need you to help us in the vineyards. You can drive Kit and rake out the brush."

"Oh, Pa, can I?" I never have been asked to do this before. I'm thrilled. I love driving the Belgian workhorses. We have two teams, Jim and Dan and Kit and Bess. I usually drive Bess but I know she was used yesterday and needs to rest today.

"Yes," Pa says. "Here it is the first of April and we don't have the grapes trimmed. It has rained almost every day. The fields are a nasty, muddy mess. The teams are muddy and we are muddy. I detest spring for all its mud."

"Please wash before you say another word, Charles. Dinner is ready. Here is some nice warm water for you."

"Thank you, Ellen." Doc and Uncle Ed nod their thanks. Uncle Ed is Pa's youngest brother. He is a little taller than Pa and very thin. His eyes are blue and he has dark hair.

"It sure smells good in here, Missus," Doc says with a gleam in his eye. The hard-working men enjoy the delicious food Ma and Ruthie prepare. There is always plenty to eat at our house.

After we are all seated at the dining table, Pa says to me, "Wear your oldest work clothes and the old slicker with the holes in it. It is not raining much now but it will keep the wind off you. The rain could begin again."

"Yes, Pa." I stuff myself with as much food as I can hold. It's going to be a long cold afternoon.

In my room I put on my wool underdrawers, old wool vest Ruthie had knitted for me, flannel shirt, and corduroy pants. These were school pants but they are too worn for school.

In the woodshed I struggle into my old patched coveralls and patched coat with the frayed cuffs. The clothes are tight. Good. That means I have grown some. I pull the felts from my boots and make sure there aren't any pebbles stuck in them. I sure don't want to spend the afternoon walking with a stone in my boot. After pulling the horse hair fibers together to close several holes I replace the felts in my boots and jump in ready for work.

As we walk to the barn to get Kit, Pa gives me instruction, "You must be very careful directing your horse, Danny. Work slowly and carefully. Try to do a clean job but if you miss a few of the cut pieces of vine here and there that is all right. The important thing, as you know, is to not damage the vines or posts."

"Yes, sir. I'll be very careful."

"Just leave the piles of brush at the end of each row. Doc is trimming and Ed is pulling brush. You will rake and I will pick up the piles and take them to be burned. We will make good progress with four of us working together. The bullrake is outside the equipment shed. I'm sure you know that is what the brush rake is also called. I'll help you harness Kit then you are on your own."

"Yes, Pa," I say with a smile. Oh boy, except for the cold and wet mud this work is going to be fun to do, and I will be helping my family a lot. I have not done this work before but have seen the men do it. Kit has done this chore so she will not need much guidance, just when we turn around at the end of each row and start the next. She certainly knows more about raking brush than I do.

The brush rake is lying on the wet ground by the door to the equipment shed. The rake is lying close to the building so no one will step on it. It is just a length of thick plank about five feet long with large metal spikes sticking through it. Each end has a skid to raise the rake off the ground a few inches. Now it is upside down with the spikes and skids pointing up. I will have to turn it over when Kit and I start down the first row in the vineyard.

Oh, no. It has just occurred to me. Will I be able to flip the heavy oak plank right side up? The men will be nearby but I don't want to ask for help. I will do it I say to myself with determination. I shackle one end of the plank to the single tree so it can be pulled to the vineyard the men are working in.

"Giddap, Kit. Lets go to work." I am glad to be moving as it is windy, cold, and damp. It will be hard to keep warm.

CHAPTER 2

▼

WORKING IN THE VINEYARDS

My joy in being a help to my family is soon greatly decreased by the difficulty of walking in the mud. The lane is very muddy. There are large puddles every few feet. My boots are quickly coated with thick globs of soggy muck. It is difficult for me to lift my feet. I struggle along the lane to the Concord vineyard where the men are working. Once I am on the grass and weeds of the vineyard I can scrape off most of the mud.

A quick glance shows me where Doc and Uncle Ed have already worked so that is where I begin. I start Kit down the space between the first and second row of vines on the west side of the vineyard.

"Whoa, girl." She stands while I attempt to turn over the rake. I must be able to do this. Kit is looking at me over her left shoulder and I am sure the men are watching too. I grasp in the center and with a mighty heave flip the heavy plank onto its skids.

I am a success! What a great feeling. Doc, who is the nearest to me is watching my efforts. He gives me a big grin to acknowledge my victory over the heavy plank.

I attach the free end of the rake to the singletree, take up the reins and call, "Giddap, Kit." She continues between the rows and I plod along behind the rake. I very carefully watch to make sure an end of the plank doesn't hit a grapevine or post. Ah, raking is quite easy I think to myself. Easy until I reach the end of the row and I must leave the pile of brush behind. How do I get the rake over or around it?

"Whoa, Kit." I stand looking at the rake and the pile of brush.

Pa sees my hesitation and comes striding to me. He asks, "What's the matter?" He is not smiling.

"How do I get the rake past the brush pile?"

"Take the shackle off this end of the plank and direct your horse ahead until the rake is clear of the pile. It will swing clear as Kit pulls it ahead. That was how it was attached when you left the shed. Then reshackle the free end. See how this end is meant to be easily removed from the hitch?" He looks at me as if I should have known this.

"Oh, yes, I understand. Thanks Pa."

"You're welcome." He looks down the row I just raked. "Good job," and goes back to pulling brush with Uncle Ed until I have enough raked into piles for him to pitch onto the hay wagon with a heavy fork meant for that purpose. When he has a load, he will cart it off to be burned when it is dry.

Except for the wet weather and the mud, it is a good day to be working outside. I do my best not to get wet and muddier. In the vineyard the ground is mostly covered by grass and weed plants but many have not revived themselves from the cold of winter. The grass and some of the weeds are turning green and it is nice to see the bright color after the dullness of winter. There are still snow and ice patches in some places. I step in these areas whenever possible to avoid the mud.

The grape plants, where the men have not yet worked, are a tangle of dark brown dormant vines. Doc is doing the most import work in the vineyard, trimming the vines. He carefully studies each one before he snips away the unwanted growth. His goal is to have four remaining branches; two long enough to reach the top wire and two shorter shoots for the middle wire. These are called canes and will produce this year's crop of grapes.

He pulls some of the cut branches away from the wires where they were tied the year before as he works to see how he wants to shape the new growth. Trimming work will determine the amount of grapes the plant will produce. The more fruit Pa has the sell the more money he will make.

This money he must use to pay the mortgage on our farm and purchase goods for our family for an entire year. Of course the farm produces other income during the year, but nothing close to the amount the grape crop does. Someday Pa or Doc or Uncle Ed will show me how to properly trim our grapes.

Uncle Ed is working along the rows behind Doc completely pulling free the unwanted branches of the vine. Pulling brush is a hard job as the vines have gripped the wires in many places. They are tangled around the wire too. Care must be taken to not be struck in the face by a vine when it finally springs free.

As I direct Kit along the next row, the quiet air is disturbed by the sound of flocks of honking Canada Geese flying overhead. A few may land on Keuka Lake to rest while others continue on their way. They are flying to their summer nesting places in Canada not to be seen by us again until fall. Some will rest and eat in the Montezuma Swamp at the north end of Cayuga Lake. This Finger Lake is two lakes east of Keuka Lake.

I can't see the geese as they fly overhead because of the low clouds but I can hear them. The heavy dampness of the air muffles their calling to one another. And I can picture their huge V formation. Some groups are so low I can hear their wing beats. All the same it is a lovely and most welcome sound of spring. Even Kit lifts her head to listen.

We continue working at raking out the brush from between the rows of Concord grapevines. Pa has stopped pulling brush and is pitching the piles of vine Kit and I have left at the ends of the rows onto the hay wagon. As I walk along between the rows, I try to place my boots where they will not pick up any more mud. Not an easy task.

Then, something attracts my eye. It is an unusual shape in the dirt at the base of one of the vines. A familiar shape but not one made by nature.

"Whoa, Kit." She patiently stands while I examine the stone. It's not a stone. It's an Indian arrowhead. I wipe the mud off the flint stone the best I can on a clump of wet young grass. Yup, that is what it is. A small arrowhead for small game like rabbits. The men have found many of them while working in the fields but this is my first arrowhead. What a thrill! I quickly put it in my pocket, chirrup to Kit, and continue my work. I can't wait to show Mary, she will be excited too.

Our teacher, Miss Spaulding, has told us native people lived on Bluff Point many centuries ago. They are called the Woodland Indians and that is the name given to their arrowheads. I vow to find more information about them. We have also read about Red Jacket who was born south of Branchport on the west shore of Keuka Lake in 1758. Red Jacket was a Seneca Chief known for his speaking ability and his efforts to protect the Seneca Indian lands and culture.

The four of us men continue working the rest of the afternoon until almost dark. By mid afternoon it is softly raining again but we continue working. The grapevines must be trimmed, the brush pulled and the remaining vines tied to the wires with willow shoots before they awaken from their winter rest. If the vines are handled after the buds begin to form, many buds will be knocked off and the plant will be damaged. Buds are only formed once a year, early in the spring.

I am glad I have the old slicker to wear even if it has two holes in it. They are low and will not allow much water to reach my old coveralls.

I look up to see Ruthie coming from the house. She is walking very carefully not to get mud on her skirts which she has hiked above her boot tops. She lifts them by having the fabric tucked into a cord tied around her waist. She is bringing a welcome bucket of hot coffee for the men and some hot chocolate for me. Ruthie waits for me at the end of the row on which I am working.

"Thanks, Ruthie. Boy, it sure tastes good and warms me up some," I say gratefully.

"You are welcome, Danny. Looks like you are doing a good job."

"Thanks. It's fun but I sure have to pay strict attention."

"Oh, pooh. Kit knows what she is doing. You don't have to do anything but stay awake."

"Not so. I have to be sure she doesn't hit anything. She is good but not that good."

Ruthie laughs and starts back toward the house. She calls over her shoulder, "I did the raking a few years ago and it isn't that hard." Golly, I didn't know she had ever done such hard work. I look after her with new admiration.

As Kit and I plod along, I watch the droplets of water slowly gather on her back to form small trickles down her smooth rump. I wonder if she can feel it. If she does, she gives no sign. I think it would tickle.

The horses have begun to shed their heavy winter coat. Clumps of old fur come off as they are groomed. Kit has patches of new summer fur here and there and looks like a shaggy patch work quilt.

Later I hear the welcome words, "Hello, Danny. We are quitting for today." Pa is calling from the end of the row Kit and I just began.

"All right," I reply. Kit and I finish the row in the semidarkness and follow the men to the barnyard. Again I must clump through thick mud. My feet feel like heavy weights each time I lift one to take a step. There is a boot scraper outside the dairy barn and we take turns cleaning our muddy boots the best we can.

Pa and Uncle Ed put the rake in the equipment shed as it will not be used tomorrow. Tomorrow is Sunday and no work will be done except what is necessary for the care of the livestock and of course preparing meals.

We begin our routine chores in the dairy barn. The cows are beginning to lose their heavy winter coat of fur too. I give the two cows I take care of, Buttermilk and Sofie's underside a good rubbing to remove loose fur before I begin to milk. Ma will strain the milk through a clean cloth before it is stored but I want the milk to be as clean as possible.

I am glad to snuggle next to Buttermilk as I begin to strip the creamy fluid from her full udder into a clean two gallon pail. Her side is nice and warm. She still doesn't like me and gives me some trouble by moving about when she should be standing still.

"Soooo Buttermilk. Please be a good cow," I say as I rub her cream-colored neck. "Eat your mash and be nice to me, please." She shakes her head and goes about noisily eating. She seems more content, perhaps she doesn't dislike me as much as she did. Maybe she is just resigned to me. I hold a pail of water for her to drink then go on to milk Sofie.

Doc has finished milking his four cows and I haven't finished my two. I try to hurry. Kit needs to be groomed yet, and my very own horse to care for. I must also clean up after, feed, water, and milk my goats before supper, and I am very hungry. At least now I am warm and dry but I don't want to keep the family waiting too long for me.

"I'll take care of the horses for you, Danny," Doc says.

"Gee, thanks, Doc. Please take care of Kit. I want to work with Sally. She needs to get to know me."

"Right you are," Doc says with a quick nod of his head.

We carry the pails of steaming creamy milk to the house.

Then I go on to the basement of the horse barn where my goats live in the winter. There are six goats in all. One male who is, of course, named Billy. There are four adult females, Nellie, Gertrude, Eleanor, and Lillian. The sixth goat is a yearling and Grandpa Scott named her Olive. Adult male goats are called bucks or billies, adult female goats are called does or nannies and the young are called kids.

Olive doesn't give milk yet as she has not been bred. She is a little small but will need to be with a buck goat this spring.

Grandpa Scott said there is a man named Nathaniel Copson near Branchport that has a large dairy goat herd. He is willing to trade the services of one of his bucks for the services of my Billy. Grandpa had sold his kids to this man last year. All but Olive who was a runt and the fellow didn't want her. Grandpa and Grandma nursed her and took special care of her. Now Olive is a healthy and happy young goat.

Dairy goats eat hay like dairy cows. Alfalfa is the best for them. They are given the same mash the dairy cows receive. Pa uses our wind-mill-powered mill to grind corn, barley, and buckwheat for their mash. Their hay supply is kept in a rack so it stays clean as goats will not eat soiled food. Their mash is given to them in a wooden box so it remains clean until all is eaten. This way none of the valuable food is spilled on the ground and wasted.

Goats are milked like cows, twice a day, but only give about three quarts each day. Our Guernsey dairy cows give two to three gallons per day. Goats are curious and like to climb. Their pen in the basement of the horse barn has a special fence. It is high and extra strong. Billy has a pen to himself until it is time for him to be with the does.

While the goats are eating their mash, I clean out the manure and put down fresh straw. Milking is lots of fun as they are gentle and seemed to like me right away. Goats' milk is handled like cows' milk. Kept clean and cold until ready to sell or use.

I call the goats by their name and talk to them as I milk. Ruthie laughs at me about this when she catches me talking to them. I don't care, I enjoy talking to our farm animals. They are my friends.

I take the goat milk to the kitchen where Ruthie will strain it as she pours it into a milk pail for storage.

I have been saving the best chore for last, grooming my little mare. Quickly I run up the stairs to where the horse stalls are. I give Bess a pat and a hug then go to the last stall on the right where Sally is housed. Softly I call her name, "Sally, it's me, Danny. Hello, how are you? I have come to give you a good brushing and give you some oats."

Sally is a Morgan. She has distinctive markings as her left hind foot is white and she has a small white stripe down her forehead to just above her nose. Her color is called bay because she has black points. This means her mane, tail, and lower legs are black. The rest of her body is a medium brown. She stands fourteen hands high at the withers. As a hand is four inches, she is fifty-six inches high. This makes her a rather small horse.

The little mare nickers softly. Her ears are standing straight up. She seems glad to see me. I carefully brush her forelock, mane and tail until they shine. Then I currycomb her all over and give her coat a good rubbing with an old towel to make it shine too. I pay special attention to the narrow white stripe on her forehead. She is beautiful.

How long have I been grooming her? I ask myself. I better give her some oats and hay and get to the house. Supper must be ready and everyone will be waiting for me.

It is totally dark by the time I rush to the house. I can see the welcome yellow glow of lamp light through the kitchen and dining room windows. Oh, oh, I have really done it this time. I am very late.

"Where have you been, Danny?" Ma asks. "The others have been ready for supper for quite sometime."

"I, I, I had extra work to do. And I spent extra time grooming my horse. I'm truly sorry I have kept everyone waiting. It won't happen again."

"How thoughtless to keep us waiting so long," Ruthie says rapidly. "You should be ashamed. You are always late for supper."

"Please be more considerate of others," Ma says softly. "It is rude of you to keep your father and the rest of the family waiting."

"Yes, ma'am. I'm sorry, everyone," I say as I plop into my chair at the dining table. I keep my head down as I don't want to look Pa in the eye.

"Ma, aren't you going to punish him some way? You could send him to bed without his supper. That would really fix him," Ruthie says sharply.

I feel the heat of embarrassment moving rapidly up my neck and face. Mary and Carolyn are looking at me with kind sympathy. My stomach is growling from hunger, I hope Ma doesn't follow Ruthie's suggestion.

"Never you mind, Ruth. Charles, what do you think? Should we send him to bed without his supper?"

"Well, I don't know, Ellen," Pa says slowly. "Perhaps we should."

I catch Pa winking at Mary, and I know he is teasing me. We laugh and begin to pass around the food. We all laugh except Ruthie, she is pouting.

CHAPTER 3

▼

LEARNING ABOUT THE SENECA INDIANS OF LONG AGO

After supper, I show Mary the arrowhead. "Golly, what an exciting find," she exclaims. "I wish I could find one."

"You will, Sis. Just keep your eyes on the ground when you are in the fields. Pa says there are lots of them around here. The next one I find I will give to you."

"Thanks for the offer, Danny. But I want to find my own. Please show me where you found yours and I will begin to look there."

"Yes, it would be more exciting for you to find an arrowhead of your own. I think you should wait until the ground dries some. It is very difficult to walk in all the mud. I almost lost a boot today and had a hard time pulling it out of the muck."

"Oh, all right," she says with a big sigh. "I suppose the arrowheads have been there a long time and can wait a little longer for me to find."

Doc hears us talking about Indian arrowheads and says, "Well, I believe the Seneca Indians were living around the lakes long before the Revolutionary War. They did not live up here though. The arrowheads we find come from a much earlier group of people."

"Miss Spaulding has told us a little about the Woodland Indians," I say. "She said they lived here 1000 BC to 1600 AD."

"Oh, they are called the Woodland Indians. I guess we don't know much about them," Doc says. "That sure is a long time ago. We do have some knowledge of the local Seneca Indians who lived on the shore of the lake," he continues. "They were here long before any Europeans arrived. The women grew food such as corn, squash and beans. The men hunted and fished."

"As they were farmers, they lived in villages consisting of as many as one hundred people. There were some larger villages at Geneva, Canandaigua, and Kashong on the west shore of Seneca Lake. There was another large village south of Rochester, near Victor."

"After they made contact with the Europeans they learned to grow apples, peaches, pears, potatoes and had pigs and chickens. The people lived in longhouses made of a framework of poles and covered with tree bark. Several families lived together in the longhouses. Wigwams were temporary dome shaped houses."

"But how did they stay warm in the winter?" I ask.

"They kept fires going inside the longhouses. There was an opening in the roof over each fireplace to let out the smoke and let in some light. These fires were used for heat and cooking just as we do today. A bear skin or deer skin was used as a door flap. They wore warm clothing made of deer skin and had blankets of bear skin."

"Boy, they sound very interesting," I exclaim.

Doc says, "They must have lived quite well and happily within their family groups or clans. The children and old folks were well taken care of. Each family member, when old enough, had a job to do and contributed to the welfare of the whole group."

"Perhaps there were Indians living close to where Captain Williamson had his place," Doc continues. "I hear tell there is an Indian family living somewhere over on the west branch of the lake near Branchport. Perhaps they are still there. You might look for them and ask them about Indian families living up here in the old times."

"That is a good idea, Doc. Teacher says Red Jacket was born over there someplace. I'll do some exploring when the roads dry and I have more time. I'll ride my mare. In the spring there is lots of grape work to do, and I want to help as much as I can."

"Right you are, Danny," Pa says. "We can use your help after school. I know you would like to have time to ride your horse but work must come first."

"It's all right, Pa. I understand." I am disappointed but family concerns must come before individual wants. I'm not much help trimming the apple, cherry, and peach trees and can only pick up the brush. The trimmers must stand on ladders and being tall helps a lot. Tall I am not.

"Good boy," says Pa as he gives me a little hug.

Ma comes into the family parlor and asks, "When will you be going into town next, Charles? Easter is this month and Danny needs a new suit and the girls need new shoes. I do not want the children to go to church on Easter looking like ragamuffins."

"Yes, all right Ellen. We will pay a visit to the Davis Brothers. I'll slaughter one of the brood sows. Jacob or Louis Davis will surly take part of it in payment for Danny's suit. I'll sell the rest at the Habberfield Meat Market and have the cash for the girl's shoes. I must go to the Sheriff's office tomorrow. Is there anything you need before Saturday?"

"No," Ma says.

"Why do you have to go to town tomorrow?" Ruthie asks.

"I must give a statement about what happened on the train while we were traveling to Gorham. The Yates County Sheriff has been asked by the Ontario County Sheriff to collect information about the horrible incident. I will be giving a deposition. That is a sworn statement about what happened to Mary and Danny. By doing this now perhaps we won't have to go to court in Canandaigua."

"Oh, Pa, I hope I don't have to go to court," wails Mary.

"I hope you don't either," says Pa sadly.

"I'll go to Canandaigua to speak to the court if you go with me Pa." I say bravely. "I want to tell the judge how that evil man picked my sister up by her feet and hit me twice when I tried to help her. That man had wicked ideas and I think he should be kept in jail. Don't you think he should be in jail, Pa?"

"Yes I definitely do."

"Golly, I don't want to be in court in Canandaigua but I will go if you say it is necessary."

"Thank you, Danny. I hope our going to court won't be necessary."

"Pa, you can have Olive to sell. Please don't kill one of the sows," I plead. Tears are coming to my eyes and my throat hurts. I must not cry here in front of everyone. I don't want to sell poor little Olive but we need the brood sows so we will have young pigs to sell later when they will bring a good price.

"Charles, we have quite a lot of butter and cheese. The hens are laying more now. Why can't we sell these to Dr. Ball at the college? Then we won't need to sell any stock."

"Good idea, Ellen. We have a forequarter of frozen beef too. We will try the college first and if they don't take it all I'm sure I can trade the rest with the Davis Brothers."

"Thank you for your offer to sell Olive, Danny. She will be of much more value to you when she can have kids. There are times to sell adult livestock. The brood sows are getting past their prime and will have to go after this spring anyway. Olive will provide income from milk and as a brood doe for at least seven years. You must not throw that away."

We will all go to Penn Yan when we finish the grape work. Ellen, please check your supplies of flour and cornmeal. If need be, we will draw some from our account at the Birkett Mills."

Mary and Carolyn chorus together, "To town we will go, new shoes we will get." They hold hands and skip around in a circle repeating their song and add, "Heigh-ho a merry-o, to town we will go."

"Girls, girls, you know better than to run in the house," Ma exclaims.

"Yes, ma'am, we're sorry," Mary says. She and Carolyn are still holding hands but have stopped skipping and are looking at the floor. They are embarrassed for having been reminded not to run in the house.

"Good girls," Ma says with a smile. "It is time for you to get ready for bed."

"Yes, ma'am," Mary replies.

Carolyn is pouting and says, "But I don't want to go to bed now."

Mary takes Carolyn by the hand and says, "Come on, I'll read to you from our *Mother Goose* book."

"Oh, goodie," exclaims the little girl. "That will make going to bed fun. Which poems will you read?"

"I don't know, you can pick them," Mary says with a big smile. She is confident she will be able to read any *Mother Goose* rimes in our book her little sister picks.

Ruthie says, "Both of you jump in bed and I'll read *The Children's Hour* to you."

"*The Children's Hour*? What is that?" Carolyn asks. Mary looks puzzled too.

"It's a poem by Henry Wadsworth Longfellow," I say. "You'll like it. Miss Spaulding said Mr. Longfellow wrote the poem for his children. I want to hear it too, Ruthie."

"All right, get ready for bed and I'll be up in a few minutes."

"Thank you, big sister," we say together.

We meet on Mary's bed. "How many children did Mr. Longfellow have, Ruthie?" Mary asks.

"I think I read his family consisted of two boys and three girls. The poem was published in 1860 in a magazine called *The Atlantic Monthly*."

"That is a long time ago," Carolyn exclaims.

"Sure is," smiles Ruthie. She begins to read:

Between the dark and the daylight,

the night is beginning to lower,
    Comes a pause in the day's occupations
        That is known as the Children's Hour.

The next thing I know Ruthie is shaking my shoulder. "Get up sleepy head and go to your own bed. The girls are asleep and I didn't even finish the poem."

"How far did you get?" I ask quietly as I slide off Mary's bed.

"Only to the beginning of the castle part. Good night, Danny."

"Good night, Ruthie." I slip into my bed and am soon asleep.

Sunday morning arrives and we have our last family meal with Miss Spaulding. Pa and Uncle Ed load her trunk and bags onto the hay wagon. I find Mary and Carolyn in tears over teacher leaving. "It is silly for you to feel sad about Miss Spaulding not living with us anymore," I say. "We will see her at school each day."

"It won't be the same. She won't read to us anymore and she won't be around to talk to when we want," Mary wails.

"I won't see her anymore, ever," little Carolyn cries.

"Oh, yes you will, you will be starting school in the fall and Miss Spaulding will be your teacher," I say as I give her a little hug.

"Goodie, goodie, I will be going to school too. I forgot about that. How far away is fall, Danny?"

"About five months."

"Five months, that is forever," Carolyn cries loudly in despair.

"Yes, you will need to be very patient."

Pa calls from the kitchen, "Children, come on now, it's time to go to Sunday School."

After Sunday School Pa, Uncle Ed, and Mr. Marshall transfer teacher's belongings to his wagon.

We wave good-bye as teacher is driven away. She turns in her seat, waves to us, and blows a kiss. Who did she blow the kiss to, I wonder? She wouldn't blow a kiss to us I don't think.

As I turn to walk to our wagon, I see Uncle Ed, with his hands deep in his trouser pockets, watching Mr. Marshall's wagon goes around the bend in the road and out of sight. Miss Spaulding was blowing the kiss to him. He walks dejectedly to our wagon and slowly climbs on. Pa gives him a pat on the shoulder as he chirrups to the team.

After school each day, I work with the men in the vineyards until dark. Ma and Ruthie are working there too. They are helping with the tying of the canes to the wires. The tiers carry a supply of willows in a bundle on their back in a canvas sling.

And when we come in for a late supper, Mary and Carolyn have hot food ready for us. Vineyard work is truly a family effort. It sure feels good to know I am a part of it.

At first, I use Bess or Kit to rake brush. When that is finished, I use the stone boat to supply the tiers with willows. It is difficult for me to lift the bundles of willows onto the stone boat but I do it. We work together in the damp cold of early April. Finally we finish the vineyard work and it is time to plan our trip to Penn Yan on Saturday.

It is a big event for us to go to town together. Proudly our parents will walk along the streets of Penn Yan, side by side, and we children will tag along behind.

First I need to ride Sally to Keuka College to ask Mr. Ehule if his kitchen needs beef, eggs, cheese or butter. I have not ridden her much and never before away from home. Pa helps me get ready.

He reminds me, "Your horse does not yet know our farm is where she lives now and you have had little experience riding. If you are thrown off, she probably will not come home and will be lost. Or perhaps she will go back to the Argyle place. Do you understand?"

"Yes, sir. I will be very careful and keep Sally under control at all times. And I will not let my mind wander from my riding."

"All right, Danny. See that you do." Pa gives me a leg up and my horse starts forward. I urge her into a trot.

Pa's old saddle is too big for me, and I have a difficult time staying in place. Pa tied a rolled up empty grain sack to the front of the cantle and that helps some. The stirrup leathers are adjusted to their shortest but are still a little too long.

I guide Sally right onto the Ridge Road and we are on our way to Keuka Park and Keuka College. It is about a twelve-mile round trip. I'm thrilled to be able to ride Sally so far.

I'm worried about having to talk to Mr. Ehule in the college kitchen. He looks mean and I don't think he will talk to me. He didn't even talk to my Pa. If he didn't want to talk to my Pa why would he speak to me, I wonder. Well, I will do my best and hope everything works out. In the meantime I will enjoy my trip on my very own horse. We move smoothly north on the Ridge Road.

What a pleasure it is to ride a horse that isn't a draft horse. Of course I still love good old Bess.

CHAPTER 4

▼

MY FIRST LONG RIDE ON SALLY

Riding Sally is wonderful but talking to her is not like talking to my old friend Bess. As much as I say to her, it doesn't result in any ear wiggles.

"Sally, how do you like my riding you?" I ask. "It's got to be better than having Mr. Argyle on your back. I weigh a lot less. I'm going to treat you very gently. You and I can become real pals. Right now you probably don't understand you are my horse. Soon we will be true friends. We will go to lots of places together and explore all over Bluff Point. I want to find Captain Charles Williamson's campsite and the home of the Indian family Doc mentioned."

Still no response from Sally. I share my thoughts and concerns about Mr. Ehule with her anyway. My horse takes no notice of my words. She just keeps trotting along. "Please be my friend, Sally." She just has to be my friend. I'll think of something else.

Perhaps Mr. Ehule won't be in the school kitchen and there will be another person to speak with about the food items we have for sale. That will be good, but another person could be scary too. My mind keeps jumping around and I am becoming ever more nervous. I must stop thinking about what might happen and concentrate on what is happening now.

It is a perfect day to be out riding. I will take joy in that. There is little wind and the sky is a beautiful clear blue. I have on my second-best winter coat and heavy brown corduroy knickers. My dark blue knit hat is pulled down over my ears. My flannel shirt is blue check. These are my school clothes.

My eyes are tearing a little because of the speed of my horse and the cold. At this rate, it won't take long to arrive at the college. Then I must face the sinister Mr. Ehule.

I slow my horse to a walk as we move through the community of Bluff Point. Two people are standing outside the Post Office at Kinney's Corners. I wave as I ride up to the Post Office and the people wave back. One person is Mr. Barrow who is a merchant at Kinney's Corners. My Pa buys his poultry from him sometimes. The other person I recognize as the Post Master, Mr. Moore.

"Mr. Moore, do we have any mail, please?" I ask.

"No, Danny, I don't think so. I'll go check your box to be sure." The postmaster quickly steps into the post office. He returns in a moment.

"The box is empty. Sorry you don't have any mail. At least there is no bad news." Mr. Barrow nods his head in agreement with this statement.

"Yes, sir. Thank you Mr. Moore. Perhaps we will have a letter next week," I say hopefully.

"Could be," Mr. Moore says. "Some folks around here get a letter every week."

"Do tell," Mr. Barrow exclaims. "And who might they be?"

"I'm not telling you, the mail is private you know."

"The inside is private. Anyone can see what is written on the outside," Mr. Barrow states.

"The outside is nobody's business but the person who wrote the letter and the one who receives it. I'm the postmaster and I ought to know." Mr. Moore is quite excited by this time. "I'm not going to go around talking about everyone's mail and that's final."

"Whooeee, ain't you something special," Mr. Barrow declares loudly.

All this loud talk is making me nervous so I change the subject by asking Mr. Barrow how his chickens and turkeys are this spring.

"Doing just fine young Lee. Your Pa going to buy some is he?"

"Ahhh, I don't know, Sir."

"Where are you off to riding your fine horse?" Mr. Barrow asks sharply.

"I am on my way to the college to speak to Mr. Ehule for my Pa."

"That old buzzard. He sure is a strange one. Never talks to anyone as far as I know," Mr. Moore exclaims. "Doesn't even talk to me when he comes for his mail. What little mail he gets. Hope he talks to you. May I ask what are you going there for?"

I nervously play with my horse's reins. "Farm business. We have some stuff to sell," I say as I smile and try to look unconcerned.

"Oh, well, good luck. You're going to need it," Mr. Moore says dramatically. The two men walk away speaking quietly to each other. Then I hear, "I hope that boy will be all right with that crazy man."

Now I am even more concerned about dealing with Mr. Ehule.

My ride to the college continues to be uneventful. I keep rehearsing in my mind what I am going to say to the creepy man I must do business with. Good day to you, sir. It's a grand day today don't you think? You are looking well. Would you care to see my horse? No, none of these seem to fit Mr. Ehule. My heart sinks. My meeting with this strange man is going to be awful. How am I going to begin my conversation with him?

I arrive at the school and carefully direct Sally to the kitchen entrance. It is on the south end of the huge building. I slide off the mare and tie her to the hitching post outside the kitchen door.

My banging on the door with my fist doesn't bring a response so I cautiously push the door open and step into the dark hallway. The door swings shut behind me with a heavy thud and I am left alone in the dark. I try not to panic.

"Hello, is there anyone here?" I call loudly. I want very badly to turn and leave but know I can't. I am here on an important errand for my Pa that may result in enough money to buy shoes for the girls and a suit for me. A strong feeling of uneasiness almost overwhelms me. My palms are sweaty and my legs are trembling so it feels like my knees are knocking together. I try to shrug off my fear.

I call again only louder, "Hello, is there anyone here?" My voice seems to go nowhere. But this time I hear slow shuffling steps coming toward me. Suddenly I see the dim light from a candle and Mr. Ehule's pinched face lit behind it. I about jump out of my skin. A chill runs down my back. He is even more scarey looking then I remember. If he were not standing, I would think he was dead. His face sure looks dead. Why is his body twisted to the left?

"Good afternoon, Mr. Ehule," I say nervously. "A fine day don't you think?"

"What are you doing here?" Mr. Ehule asks in a high-pitched voice that fits his small twisted body. He does talk after all. This gives me some confidence.

"Umm." My mouth is dry and I can barely speak. "My Pa sent me to ask you if the college needs any beef, eggs, cheese or butter, sir."

"I don't like young'uns traipsing around in my kitchen."

"I knocked on the door but no one answered. I'm very sorry if I did something wrong, Mr. Ehule."

"Who are you? What are you doing here? Who gave you permission to come here?" His little dark eyes appear to be looking right through me. They stand out starkly against his gray white skin. "Youngsters shouldn't be out and about alone. They can't be trusted."

More fear grips my stomach. "Mr. Ehule, I'm Danny Lee and my father, Charles Lee, introduced me to you a few weeks ago. I've come to ask if you need any food supplies from our farm."

"Oh, well, I see, that explains your presence here," Mr. Ehule says slowly. "I remember now. I would rather do business with your father. I don't like children. Where is he?" His voice is sharp and demanding. It is even higher in pitch. His expression is cold and calculating.

"He is at home, working. He sent me in his place."

Oh golly, this man gives me the willies. I try to smile but know it won't work. My face feels like it will crack. I'm scared as I have never been scared before. I must do this. I must not be afraid of Mr. Ehule. What is there to be afraid of? I ask myself. Plenty is my answer.

"Oh, well, come along then. My room is down this hall. I'll talk to you there," he says gruffly.

"Yes, sir. Thank you, sir." I hope my voice doesn't sound as afraid as I feel. The misshapen man leads me along the dim hall. There are no widows. We come to a small room. A rumpled bed is in one corner. Another corner holds a small wardrobe. The doorway takes up almost an entire wall. Against the fourth wall are two wooden crates with a plank across to make a table of sorts. An old heavy wooden chair stands next to the table.

The flickering light of the candle reveals a small window high on the wall over the bed. It is covered with a heavy drape. It lets in no outside light. It is like Mr. Ehule is afraid of the light as I am afraid of the dark.

After we enter the room, Mr. Ehule turns to face me. "Now, boy, tell me again why you are here. Speak up as I am a little hard of hearing."

"Yes, sir." My voice cracks as I speak. "My Pa has sent me to ask you if the college needs any beef, butter, cheese or eggs. My Ma has some extra she would like to sell." I hope I don't sound as nervous as I feel. A trickle of sweat goes down my back.

"Well, I don't rightly know. Let me think." Mr. Ehule blinks his small eyes a couple of times. His forehead is wrinkled like it is a great effort for him to think.

My hope is fading. Have I come here for nothing? If I have, where will we get the money for the items we need?

What if this strange man won't let me leave? What if he locks me in this dark room? I must not think such things but they keep popping into my head. Mr. Moore called him crazy. I remember what my friend Stan said, that this curious man might be a thief or a kidnapper. Or worse. Maybe he murders children. He says he doesn't like them. Oh golly, I'm frightened! I can feel my legs trembling.

"What did you say your name was again?" Mr. Ehule's gaze is fixed on me. His face is only inches away from mine. His teeth are broken and yellow. Tobacco stained, I guess.

"Lee, sir. Danny Lee. My father sent me here." I know my voice must be quavering.

"Oh, yes, I remember now," he says again. Mr. Ehule slowly sinks onto the chair. He reaches out with his shriveled hand and touches my hand. My body goes cold. I want to withdrawal my hand but don't dare. His hand is like ice. The odor of cooked food is on his clothes. My brain says RUN! My legs say I can't.

Mr. Ehule finally says, "Of course, what a good idea. I do believe we are almost out of those items. In fact our larder is almost bare. How much is your Pa asking?"

I manage a weak smile and say, "The beef is six cents a pound, cheese is ten cents a pound, the butter is fifteen cents a pound and the eggs are twelve cents a dozen."

"Them prices are mighty dear, boy." Mr. Ehule is giving me a squinty eyed look. My knees are shaking. What do I say?

"Perhaps we can strike a bargain if the college takes our entire stock," I say tentatively. "My Ma has eight pounds of cheese, twelve pounds of butter and ten dozen eggs. We have a forequarter of fine beef that weighs eighty-two pounds. We can make delivery first thing Saturday morning." I say all this quickly trying to sound businesslike.

"Lets do some ciphering." The strange man fumbles among the papers on his make shift table and finds a stub of a pencil. He smooths some wrinkles from a scrap of paper and proceeds to do his calculations. In a moment he hands me the paper. "Do you agree with this?" he asks sharply.

By the flickering candle light I carefully work the multiplications and addition. A mistake here would be a disaster. I agree with his total of eight dollars and seventy-two cents. A magnificent sum. I hope it is enough to make our purchases. Perhaps there will be money left over to buy a pair of shoes or something else for Ma.

I say smartly, "Yes, sir, I agree with your calculations."

"Go home and tell your Pa that I offer to pay eight dollars and fifty cents for his goods. And not a penny more. I'll see you to the door."

"Yes, sir, Mr. Ehule. Thank you."

An uncontrolled shudder goes down my back as I move along the dark hall. I can hear Mr. Ehule shuffling behind me. He is close to me. The candle light is dim but causes a huge shadow on the walls before me. I know it is my shadow but it is spooky all the same. Soon I can see light through the cracks around the door that leads outside. I quickly fumble with the latch. The fearsome man is right behind me. His breath is slow and labored. I want desperately to escape. His arm comes across my body and works the door latch.

I push the door open and say, "Good-bye, Mr. Ehule and thank you, I'll see you first thing Saturday morning." He nods his head but says nothing.

Golly I'm glad to be outside the building in the sunlight again. The kitchen door closes behind me but I still have the picture of Mr. Ehule's pale face and small dark eyes in my mind. Jeepers, I'm glad to be away from that terrible man.

I'm so happy to see Sally standing by the hitching post. But again she acts as if she doesn't know me. My heart sinks. I hope this horse will be as friendly toward me as Bess and Kit are. They would have greeted me in some way. My little mare doesn't even turn her head toward me. Perhaps it is as Pa says, it will just take sometime. I very much want it to be soon.

Well, I can't think of this now. I have more important things to think about. Hopefully my Pa will like the arrangements I made with Mr. Ehule.

By standing on the big block of stone next to the hitching post I can mount my horse easily. "Giddap, Sally, lets go home," I say as I touch my heels to her sides. She responds immediately and steps out smartly.

Three young ladies are walking toward me along the lane that leads away from the college building. I use all my leg strength to firmly hold my seat as I urge Sally into a steady trot. The young ladies are watching me and my horse. The horse is beautiful. Now if I can look good setting on her.

I manage a confident smile as I ride by, at least I think I look confident. The young ladies smile and wave. I turn in the saddle and smile and wave back. One girl looks younger than the others and is waving again. I wonder who she is? She doesn't look old enough to be going to school here. Her blond hair is in tight ringlets. She is very pretty. Wait a minute. What am I doing thinking about a girl? Yikes!

Look like you know what you are doing. I must pay attention to my horse and think about the girl later. Now I must concentrate on my riding. No mistakes, please. Pa says the character of a man can be seen in how he rides and takes care of his animals and family.

I feel better now that my first meeting alone with Mr. Ehule is over. He sure is a strange fellow. It gives me the willies just to think about my being alone with him in the dark basement of the college. I relax in the saddle and hope the ladies didn't see it is too big for me.

I wonder what Pa will say about the financial arrangement Mr. Ehule offered? Pa didn't tell me I could accept less than the full price of the goods. I hope he agrees with the offer right away as I don't want to talk to that strange man again. It would be grand if we can drop off the goods on our way to town and receive payment then. I don't know anything about the business of being a farmer. There is a lot to learn. Pa will help me I'm sure.

Sally and I go past the Assembly Grounds and I wonder what kind of programs they will have there this summer. Lots of nice ones no doubt. There will be beautiful music, dance, and speechifying. The bad part about going to an Assembly Meeting is that we must be in our best clothes and on our best behavior.

We turn left onto the Ridge Road and as we must ride up the long steep hill, I guide Sally to a walk. I talk to her and pat her neck. Again she ignores me.

When Sally and I arrive home, our dog Buster runs and noisily greets us in our lane. Buster is a black and white collie. He has long fur, white down his chest, feet and tail tip. Buster does several of his usual greeting back flips and frightens Sally. My horse shies a little and side-steps but I don't have any trouble quieting her.

"Buster, get away," I say. He lets out several sharp barks at Sally, and she sidesteps again. She wants to run but I won't let her. My firm control of the reins tells her to stand. She responds well to my commands but continues to be afraid of Buster. I can feel her nervous energy under me.

Pa walks toward us and calls Buster away from my horse. She settles down then. "How was your trip to the college? Did you have any trouble?" he asks. He gives Sally a pat on the neck.

"The ride down and back was very enjoyable," I say as I slide off my horse. "Sally behaved very well and is a pleasure to ride. Her gait is wonderful." Pa is holding her head and patting her muzzle.

"Yes, I thought so when I rode her at the Argyle place," Pa says.

"You rode her?"

"Of course, you didn't think I would take a horse in payment of a debt without seeing how it handled did you? Especially since I was going to give the horse to an inexperienced rider like you."

"Oh, Pa, I'm experienced, I have ridden Bess a lot and Andy and Toby some."

"Yes, I agree, but your experience riding alone is very limited. Controlling a true riding horse is different from riding a draft horse. What came of your talk with Mr. Ehule?"

"My, that man is strange," I say quietly.

Buster is nudging his head under my arm, asking to be petted. I give his ears a quick rub. He is wiggling all over with pleasure.

"That he is but you must not treat him any differently than you would anyone else," Pa says sternly.

"Yes, sir, I understand. He gives me the willies though. I was alone with him in that dark basement."

"Does he wish to buy our goods?" Pa's voice shows his impatience and brings me to the business at hand.

"Yes he does. He will buy the entire lot. I gave him the price and he offered eight dollars and fifty cents. That is twenty-two cents less than the proper total. Is that all right?"

"Yes, of course, you did good, Danny. I'm very proud of you. Your first business transactions were a success."

"Well, I really didn't do much. I told Mr. Ehule we would deliver the goods early Saturday morning."

"That is fine, Danny. Groom your horse and do the rest of your chores. It's almost supper time. Please do try to be prompt this time," he says with a broad smile.

"Yes, Pa. I will." I quickly change into my work clothes and manage to get all my usual barn chores done before supper time. My folks don't have to wait for me today.

CHAPTER 5

▼

FAMILY TRADING IN PENN YAN

It is Saturday at last. Ruthie, Mary and Carolyn are excited about our trip to Penn Yan. It is always exciting to go to town. The prospect of new shoes is almost unbearable for them. Ruthie, of course, is trying to hide her excitement for she thinks of herself as a young lady and thus above it all.

I'm excited too for I am to have a new suit for Easter. Ma and Ruthie have been busy remaking one of Ruthie's old dresses for Mary and making one of Mary's old dresses over for Carolyn. Ruthie has the new dress she made during the winter when she and Miss Spaulding worked together at dressmaking.

I wish Ma had a new dress too. Pa says there should be enough money left from buying my suit and shoes for the girls for us to purchase fabric or shoes for Ma. We hope so.

Pa has swept most of the dirt out of the democrat wagon and placed the extra seat inside. Now the six of us can travel in style. We have a large load of produce to take to Keuka College but all of us can squeeze in the wagon. Our picnic lunch is in a basket on my lap.

The next time the family travels to town we should be able to go by lake steamer. Then we will use the *Cricket* or the *Earl* to go to town. Together the two boats are called the Lee Line and carry freight and passengers between Branchport and Penn Yan. Travel by steamboat is still impossible early in April as the ice has not left the north ends of Keuka Lake. Branchport and Penn Yan are still iced in at some places.

Mary and Carolyn play *Pat-A-Cake* during our ride to Keuka Park and the college. They clap each other's hands and knees in time with the rhyme.

> Pat-a-cake, pat-a-cake,
> Baker's man!
> So I do, master,
> As fast as I can.
>
> Pat it, and prick it,
> And mark it with T,
> Put it in the oven
> For Tommy and me.

Sometimes they say our names or the names of school friends in place of Tommy. This makes everyone laugh. We stop at the post office at Kinney's Corners to see if there is any mail for us.

"I want to get the mail," Mary says brightly.

"I'll go with you," Carolyn chimes in.

"All right Missy, you and Carolyn may get our mail," Pa says. "I doubt whether there is any but you may try."

I jump off the wagon and help the girls down. They go gaily skipping into the post office. Shortly they come back out walking slowly. A look of concern is on their faces. A white envelope is in Mary's hand. She brings it to the wagon and hands it to Pa.

"It is from your mother, Ellen. Do you want me to open it?" Pa's voice is very quiet.

"Yes, please. Oh dear, I hope nothing is wrong. Otherwise why would she write? We were just with them two weeks ago. Heavens, what if the move was too much for my Papa? Perhaps brother Ed or

John were injured by a horse while fitting a shoe." Ma's voice is quavering.

Pa says softly, "Please calm yourself, Ellen, and stop thinking of the worst. Lets see what your Mama has to say."

Ma and Pa have worried looks on their faces. Carolyn is beginning to cry. Mary looks at me with tears in her eyes and I see her swallow hard. I try to look brave. Pa carefully opens the envelope with his pocket knife and soon has a big smile. He hands the letter to Ma.

Ma quickly reads the letter to herself and says, "It's a thank-you letter from your grandpa and grandma, children." Relief is in her voice and a smile on her face.

"Oh, goodie, please read it out loud, Ma," Mary says joyfully.

"Dearly Loved Bluff Point Folks," Ma reads. "Thank-you all for the help you gave to us during our recent move to Gorham in Ontario County. We are settled in this house and Mr. Scott has begun his new work of delivering coal to the folks here about. Our sons, John and Edward are establishing themselves as blacksmiths and help their father when they can. Daughter Minnie is still a little sad, as am I, about leaving our house on the Bluff but know we will soon call this house our home. Minnie and I have finished making the curtains for the dining room and kitchen. They look very nice. Please come and visit us during the Fourth of July Celebrations. Love from us all. Mother Scott."

"My, isn't that a beautiful letter," exclaims Ma as she wipes tears from her eyes with her best handkerchief.

"May I read it Ma?" Ruthie asks.

"Me too," Mary says.

We look at the letter and then Pa says, "We had best continue on our way."

We climb into the democrat wagon and take our seats. After Mary again reads grandma's letter for herself and little Carolyn, she looks at the stamp on the envelope.

"Did you see this stamp, Danny?" Her voice is full of excitement.

"No, who is it a picture of?"

"It's not a picture of one person. It's a picture of a group of people."

"Really, let me see." I look closely at the purple two cent stamp. "The caption says 'Landing of Columbus' across the bottom and at the top are '1492 and 1892'."

"Yes, but who are the people?"

"I imagine they are Christopher Columbus and some of his men from the ships," I say brightly.

"Oh, of course, I see. Look at the funny clothes they are wearing."

"That is how men dressed in 1492, Mary. It looks like they are glad to reach land. I think it took them thirty-three days to sail from Spain to the New World."

Pa says, "Remember, children? Mr. Huff told us about the World Columbian Exposition that was held at Chicago, Illinois in 1893. The exposition was to commemorate the four hundredth anniversary of the landing of Columbus in the New World."

We nod our heads and Pa continues, "The Exposition was held on the shore of Lake Michigan and was like a huge fair with exhibits and other attractions. That postage stamp must have been issued as part of the commemoration. I have never seen anything like it. All the other stamps I have seen have a picture of President George Washington on them."

"Isn't it pretty?" Carolyn exclaims excitedly. "It's purple," and hands the envelope back to Ma for safe keeping.

We continue on our way and Pa directs Wild Andy and Toby to the kitchen door of Keuka College. I watch the faces of Mary and Carolyn as they look at the huge four story brick building that makes up the school. They have nothing to say. They are overwhelmed by its size.

Finally Mary stammers, "I, I, I have never been close to this place before. From a distance it looks big but close up the building is huge. Just look at the bell tower!" We tip our heads back to have a good look at the bell tower which is centered on the roof.

"Yes, isn't it something?" I say quickly. I am still in awe of the building and I have been inside twice. Little Carolyn cannot think of anything to say. I hear Ma remind Carolyn and Mary that it isn't polite to stare at people because they look different. She is preparing them for when they meet Mr. Ehule. "Remember children, it is not what someone looks like that matters, it is what they do with their life."

Pa ties the reins to the wagon break lever and jumps to the ground. He raps on the kitchen door and in a few minutes Mr. Ehule comes into view. He steps outside and Pa introduces him to the family.

"How do?" is all Mr. Ehule has to say. He helps Pa and me carry the goods inside. We wave good-bye but the strange man steps into the building without looking our way.

Mary whispers to Carolyn and me, "That man is scary. Why does he look like that?"

"Dunno," I reply. "You should see him by candle light. It gives me the willies to think of it."

"How did you stand being with him? He is so scary and strange looking," Mary asks admiringly.

"Believe me, I wanted to run away but it was my duty to do business with him. So I did." I am speaking in my best grown up voice.

Mary nods her head, "That must have been difficult."

"It was."

We continue our way to Penn Yan. Pa is so happy he is humming a little tune and Ma joins in. They are happy because we are going to town together as a family. Pa is also glad he has the money to spend on my suit and shoes for the girls. Soon the whole family is happily humming together. We sing *Yankee Doodle* and *My Old Kentucky Home* which is our Ma's favorite song.

Our first stop is at Hoban's Hitching Barn on Maiden Lane where we leave Andy, Toby and the wagon.

Then it is on to the Davis Brothers Men's Furnishings store on Elm Street. We file into the store and find Mr. Jacob Davis behind the counter. He is speaking to a man standing by the cash register. Ma quickly begins to look over the boys' suits on a rack in the center of the store.

Mary whispers to me, "What does Mr. Davis mean by furnishings? He isn't selling furniture."

"In this case, Mary, furnishings means wearing apparel and accessories."

"Oh, I understand, it means suits and ties and handkerchiefs."

"Yes, that's right."

Mr. Davis crosses the room and speaks to Pa first but is keeping a sharp eye on Ma, "Welcome to our store, Mr. Lee. Are you interested in a suit? Or is it something for the young man?"

"A suit for the boy, Mr. Davis."

"Ah, I see. Your Misses is looking in the right place. Those are new suits that just arrived from Rochester for spring. May I interest you in a nice twill suit for yourself? They came in also and are the latest fashion."

"No, thank you, Mr. Davis. Just a suit for our son."

I walk over to Ma and whisper, "Please may I have a dark blue suit with long pants?"

"Your Pa and I have been talking this subject over," she says with a smile. She holds a brown suit up in front of me, pressing it to my shoulders. "You know having trousers in place of knickers is a big step in your life."

"Yes, ma'am, I am ready for the change don't you think? I am not a little boy anymore. I am a responsible young man." I can see Ma smiling a little. This gives me hope. Or was she smiling because she was laughing at me for saying I am a responsible young man? I don't know.

"What do you think of this suit, Charles?" Pa walks slowly to the rack. I can see he is uncomfortable selecting a suit for me. He isn't much interested in suits.

Mr. Davis is standing to one side, his hands clasped in front of him. He is smiling pleasantly.

"Let the boy select his own suit," Pa says quietly. "Just be sure it is large enough to last him several years."

Yahoo! I say to myself. I look at Ma's face and try to see how she feels about my selecting my own suit.

"But Charles, he is just ten years old."

"Yes, that is true. He has been showing good judgment and responsibility lately and I feel he deserves to have the suit he wants."

Mary is standing at my side and I feel her poke me lightly in the ribs. She has a big smile on her face.

I whisper in her ear, "Yahoo!" She nods her head. I know she is glad for me.

"Danny, you may select the suit you want," Ma says. "I will help you with the size. We don't want you to grow out of it next year. It must last several years."

"Yes, ma'am. I understand." Oh boy, at last I can pick out my own suit. Which should I select? They all look so nice. "This one has long pants and is dark blue," I say to Mary. "What do you think?"

"It's nice but look at this one, it has white trim."

"That is called piping, Mary," Ruthie says. She is eying that one too. It is fancier than the one I am holding.

"Oh, white piping. Don't you like it, Danny?"

"Well, it's nice but it costs twenty-five cents more than this one," I whisper to the girls as I compare the two price tags. Mr. Davis is trying to show a man's suit to Ma.

"Try both on," suggests Ruthie. She likes to go shopping and knows much more about selecting an item than I do.

"How much would it cost to buy material for Ma to make a dress for herself?" I whisper to Ruthie. "I want to be sure there will be enough money for Ma to have something new too."

Ruthie says quietly, "Well, she would need four and a half yards. If we each select the least expensive shoes, and you pick a lower priced suit there surely will be enough."

"Good, that is what we will do," I whisper. Mary and Carolyn nod their agreement.

I go into the dressing room and try on the plain suit. After examining my image in the mirror, I decide this is the suit for me.

I step into the store and find all eyes are on me. My face is burning with embarrassment. I stuff my hands into the trouser pockets. They are large enough for my needs. Ma pulls my hands out and says, "Don't stretch the pocket fabric out of shape, Danny."

Mr. Davis points out the merits of the suit for Pa. Pa is nodding his head in agreement.

"Ma, please, this is the suit I would like." Ma inspects the fabric and how well the suit fits me.

"Raise your arms over your head," she demands. "Does it feel tight in the arms or across the back? Let me check the waist. Mr. Davis, what do you think about the fit? Does he have plenty of room to grow?"

"Why, yes, Mrs. Lee. Look here." He grabs the waist band and almost pulls me off my feet showing my Ma how much room there is for me to grow. Then he spins me around and shows Ma how much loose fabric there is in the back of the jacket. "See the sleeves and trousers are about two inches too long. Yes, ma'am, I would say he has plenty of room to grow. Does the young man have a tie and hat to go with his new suit?"

"My old ones will do just fine, Mr. Davis," I say quickly before Ma gets any ideas about buying a new hat or tie for me.

"Ma, the pockets are a good size and seem strong." She nods her agreement. Pockets are important to me. I never know what I might want to put inside them.

Pa steps up and gravely asks, "What do you think about the size, Ellen?"

"It is good. The suit should last him for several years if he doesn't grow terribly fast."

Of course, I hope I will grow fast. My image in the dressing room mirror is pitifully small. I admire the suit and note how soft the fabric is. And best of all, it has trousers like the men wear.

"Danny, do you like this suit? Or do you want to try on the other one?" Ma asks seriously.

"I like this one very much. It is just what I had in mind."

"It is settled then," says a smiling Pa. "Please get out of the suit, Danny so Mr. Davis can put it in a box for us."

Oh, isn't it grand I say to myself as I look into the mirror once more. My first pair of long pants. My reflection tells me I'm grown up. I stand with my hands in my pockets admiring the suit. Will I ever be as tall and large as my Pa? I sure have a long way to go.

Pa pays Mr. Davis $4.55 for my suit. We say good-bye and thank you. Pa is carrying the big box that has my suit in it under his arm. Our next stop is the Wagener Brothers Shoe Store and factory on Seneca Street.

A little bell rings as Pa opens the door for Ma. We children file in quietly. There, standing behind the counter is the imposing figure of Mr. H. Allen Wagener. He is one of the great grandsons of Abraham Wagener, the founder of Penn Yan in 1799. I'm always in awe of the members of the Wagener Family because of their connection to the beginnings of Penn Yan and the settlement of Yates County. I wonder what it is like to be the great grandson of the founder of a town? It must be grand.

"Ah, the Charles Manley Lee family," Mr. Wagener exclaims with a smile. "Welcome to our store. We have a new stock of shoes for Easter. Fred, come to the store front, please," he calls toward the back room to his brother. "We have a family of customers."

H. ALLEN   G. FRED

"Hello," says Mr. G. Fred Wagener. "How may we serve you? How are things up on the bluff? Has anyone purchased great grandfather's old stone mansion?"

I am standing with my mouth hanging open staring at the two tall, thin Wagener brothers. They are well dressed in the latest suit fashions like we saw at the men's furnishings store.

Pa gives me a quiet reminder, "It is not polite to stare, Danny." I pretend I am interested in a pair of shoes.

"Good morning to you both," Ma says.

"Good morning," we children echo.

Pa speaks with the two store owners while Ma and the girls look over the shoes. Then the Wagener brothers come to help the girls with their selections.

"Mr. Wagner, may I see the shoe factory?" I ask.

"Of course, right this way," Mr. H. Allen Wagener says.

Pa and I have a tour of the noisy factory. I have been in it before but I never tire of studying the machinery.

Overhead are shafts, pulleys, and wide leather belts that carry the power from the stationary steam engine that is behind the factory building. Periodically, there are vertical belts that carry the power to individual machines. Men and women are sitting at these machines sewing shoes together. Some machines are used to sew the upper part and others to sew on the sole. There are even machines that punch the holes for the shoe buttons, eyes and place the buttons.

The noisy room is filled with the mixed odors of oil, grease, and tanned leather. Hanging gas lamps provide some light for the workers who are not sitting next to one of the several large but dirty windows. In another room men are cutting sheets of tanned leather into shoe parts. Their knives must be very sharp. Periodically a man stops to skillfully sharpen his knife on a whetstone.

Out of ear shot from Mr. Wagener, I say to Pa, "The shoe factory is an interesting place to work but I sure wouldn't want to be stuck inside all the time."

"I know how you feel, son. I would like to maintain the machinery but wouldn't like being inside this dark building." I nod in agreement.

Mr. Wagener ends our tour with a look at the small steam engine that powers the shoe making machines. In a shed behind the shoe factory building is a large supply of coal for the engine. As we watch, a young man shovels coal into the firebox and checks the steam pressure gauge. Mr. Wagener looks at it too and then leads us back to the store. His hands are held behind his back as if he does not want to get them dirty in the factory.

With Ma's help, the girls have selected their new shoes. Mr. G. Fred Wagener packs the shoes in their boxes and uses a stout string to tie them together. I carry the boxes by the string.

Once we are outside again, I quietly ask Pa if he has any money left.

"Yes, I do, why do you ask?"

I say, "We think it would be nice if Ma got some fabric to make an Easter dress with. Do you have enough for that?"

Pa reaches into his pocket and brings out the remaining money. "Lets see, yes, I have plenty of money for dress fabric. There will be enough to buy some nice material for your Ma. Lets go to Lown's Dry Goods store next." Ma protests our spending money for dress material for her. By the gleam in her eye we know she is pleased.

Ruthie says, "I'll help you make the dress so it will be ready for Easter. What kind of fabric are you going to get?"

"Well, I don't know. Perhaps a nice brocade if it isn't any more than thirty-five cents a yard."

"I'll help too. I can do all the basting," Mary adds.

"Thank you girls. You are always a good help."

The girls go into the store to pick out the dress fabric with Ma. Pa and I wait outside and watch the traffic flow by. Suddenly, I realize that across the street is the man who almost ran Uncle Ed and me down with his horse and carriage.

"Pa, do you see that man in the black suit and bowler hat in front of the Arcade Building?"

"Yes, who is he?"

"He is the man who almost ran Uncle Ed and me over last month."

"Are you sure?"

"Yes, I'm sure. Lets follow him and see where he is going."

"All right, find your Ma and tell her where we are going and to wait for us inside the store."

I rush inside Lown's and find Ma and the girls in the dress department. They are looking over what is offered in ready-made dresses to use as a guide for the dress they are going to make. I tell Ma what Pa said and quickly leave the store to catch up with him. It doesn't take me long to find him standing outside the Benham Hotel.

"Is he inside?" I ask breathlessly.

"Yes. After he went to his room, I asked the clerk who he is."

"Who is he?"

"He is the owner of a wine company. He is looking for vineyards to purchase in Yates County. There is a good chance he will buy your grandfather's property. His name is Mr. Overhouser."

"Do you know if he will live in the old Stone Mansion? Is his family with him? Does he have a boy my age?" I stop to get my breath.

"Whoa, son. I don't know anything about him. We will have to wait and see what happens."

"Golly, I hope he is not as inconsiderate as he seems to be."

"We don't know him yet. If his family does move to the old Wagener Mansion, we must give them time to become settled and then get to know them. We will make our judgments about them then and not before. Mr. Overhouser may be a fine fellow and have a grand family."

"If he does come from Virginia, we can learn what it is like to live there. They must see the Canada Geese in the winter," I exclaim.

"Yes, that is right. His family could have lots to offer us just as we have much to offer them. Now lets go back and find the girls. My watch and my stomach say it is time for lunch."

CHAPTER 6

▼

THE BIRKETT MILLS

Ma and the girls are waiting just inside the front door to Lown's Department Store. Ma asks, "Did you two learn any information about the stranger?"

"Yes, I did," Pa says with a mysterious look on his face, "a little." He doesn't say anything else. He is teasing Ma.

"Well, what did you learn? Honestly, Charles, sometimes you try my patience something awful." Ruthie, Mary and Carolyn are looking at Pa with rapt attention.

"Yes, Pa, what did you find out? Please don't keep us wondering," Ruthie says.

Pa smiles broadly and tells us about the visitor. "He is from the state of Virginia and makes wine and he is interested in purchasing Grandpa Scott's property for its vineyards."

"Is that all you learned?" Ma asks. "What about the house? Are you saying he doesn't care about the house?" Dismay is in her voice. It is, after all, her parent's house.

"Oh, yes, his name is Mr. Overhouser."

Ruthie asks, "What kind of name is that?"

"It's German I imagine," Pa says. He is glaring at Ruthie. "We don't care where he comes from as long as he is a decent, honest man, supports his family and cares for his livestock. Do we Miss Ruth?" Pa asks sternly.

"No Pa. I'm sorry I made reference to his heritage." Ruthie's face is red with shame.

We have been taught by our parents that what is important is how a person acts, not their heritage. If a person is a citizen of this country, he is an American. If he is not a citizen, his nationality is to be respected.

"I'm sorry but I don't know any more than what I have told you, Ellen."

We are disappointed in not learning more about the Overhouser family.

"Perhaps we could find someone in Penn Yan who knows more about the family," suggests Ruthie.

Pa says sternly, "Enough time has been spent on this subject. We will learn about the Overhouser folks if they become our neighbors."

Pa and I carry the packages to Hoban's Hitching Shed and pick up our picnic basket and milk can. The milk can had been kept in the small ice box Mr. Hoban has for himself and his patrons.

We meet Ma and the girls at the Main Street bridge. There are some benches for us to use that overlook the fast moving water in the outlet of Keuka Lake. Pa is surprised by how high the water level is. It is flowing right over the remaining ice where it is frozen to the bank. The water is the color of pea soup. A big shiver runs down my back as I think about how cold and dangerous the swift moving water is.

Mary and I walk out on the bridge and carefully lean over the railing as we often do when we are in town. The outlet is ever a source of interest to us. We don't lean out far. There, below us is the stone wall that marks the beginning of the water flow under the building across the street that helps power the Birkett Mills.

"Why is that wall there, Danny?" Mary asks.

"That is the headrace which is the beginning of the flow of water to the mill. The flume carries the water to the water wheels. A gate at the start of the flume controls the flow."

"Oh, I see. What is it called when the water has gone past the water wheels?"

"The tailrace. I'll bet the miller is using all the waterpower the mill can handle," I say.

"There sure is lots of water to use," Mary agrees.

Pa has told us the mill at this spot was started in the late 1790s. That mill building burned and was rebuilt in 1824. Much apparatus has been added and the building expanded. In these modern times,

1895, only part of the huge mill can be run by the rotating power of the two cast-iron horizontal water wheels. The rest of the mill is powered by steam engines. In times of low water flow the steam engines power the entire mill system.

It is wonderful for Penn Yan to have this mill for it isn't just a grist mill. Miss Spaulding has told us the Birkett Mills is a merchant mill which means the company grinds grain delivered from many sources and sends products to many places, even out of New York State. A grist mill is small by comparison and usually performs only local work.

I let my mind wander to the bridge we are standing on. I love looking at the beautiful arched stone work. The bridge was built of limestone blocks taken from the Crooked Lake Canal when it was abandoned in 1873. The canal was completed in 1833 and followed the route of the Keuka Lake Outlet east to Seneca Lake. We learned in school the canal wasn't fully successful. There were twenty-seven locks over its eight mile route which made travel slow. It was difficult to keep adequate water levels in the system as the canal bed leaked.

I would love to learn more about the canal, the outlet and its mills. Someday I'm going to explore the old mill sites, visit the new ones, and look at what is left of the old canal. Perhaps I will go all the way to Seneca Lake. After all, it is only six miles from Penn Yan and I have my own horse to ride.

We have had much rain and of course most of the snow and ice have melted. Mary and I look over the side of the bridge at the spillway of the dam. The dam gate is down as low as it will go. The water is flowing through the opening with a roar. It is a muddy green color with pieces of debris being carried by it. In a few places the water is flowing right over the top of the dam. As much water as possible is being let out of Keuka Lake, to go rumbling down the channel to Seneca Lake.

"The noise is kind of scary," isn't it, Danny.

"Yup. It makes me glad I am not down there."

"Me too." Mary is quiet. I know she can see in her thoughts the idea of us being swept over the dam by the powerful moving cold and dirty water.

We walk back to the benches and I see a very familiar figure coming toward us on Main Street. It is Billy Marshall. He is smartly dressed in a white shirt, his best coat and trousers. He is wearing his Sunday best on a Saturday.

"Hello, Billy. How are you? It's good to see you. Are you working for my cousin, Mr. Fenton?" Pa asks.

"Ah, it is the Lee family. Good afternoon all. Yes, sir, I'm working in Mr. Fenton's bookkeeping office today. What are you folks doing in town?"

"Good afternoon to you Billy," Ma says. "Have you had lunch?"

"We are in town to do some shopping," Ruthie explains.

"I planned to eating my lunch here," Billy says as he shows Ma his cloth sack. "It's a nice time to be outside when I have been cooped up all morning in Mr. Fenton's office. I see you have brought your lunch basket. May I join you?"

"Please do," Ma says warmly. "We have extra chocolate cake." Billy sits on the bench next to me.

"Thank you kindly," Mrs. Lee.

"How is your job? Do you still like it?" I ask.

"Oh, yes I do. It is wonderful to go to school and work a few hours after school in Mr. Fenton's accounting office. I am even taking a bookkeeping class at school. I will have a good start when I graduate from high school and begin life on my own. Mr. Fenton is helping me learn his bookkeeping methods. He told me he will soon give me a few of his smaller accounts to care for."

"That is good of him. William Fenton is a good man," says Pa. "I'm sure you are dependable help for him."

"Thank you, sir. I try to do my best," says a smiling Billy. "I have much to repay Mr. Fenton for."

"I'm sure he doesn't want any repayment, Billy."

"Perhaps not, but I will think of something I can do for him to repay his kindness."

Billy quickly eats his sandwich and we have a good talk about old times on Bluff Point. He can stay with us only a few minutes as he must be back to work. He gulps down a cup of milk and takes his cake with him. His long legs quickly carry him north on Main Street. My friend waves good-bye as he turns the corner from Main Street to Jacob Street.

"That boy will make something of himself," Pa says.

After Billy is out of sight, I ask Pa, "Do you think Uncle Philo will launch the *Earl* and *Cricket* soon?"

"Yes, I'm sure of it. The sooner he starts navigating the lake the better for his steamboat business. There is still lots of ice at Branchport where the *Earl* is because the water is relatively shallow and the ice was very thick. The Penn Yan channel where the *Cricket* is should be open soon. The fast moving water will clear out what ice there is. We will stop by the boat yard on our way home."

Oh, good, I think to myself, I always enjoy looking at the *Cricket* in the water or out.

We have delicious roast pork sandwiches, chocolate cake, and cold milk for our picnic lunch.

Across the street are the huge buildings of the Birkett Mills. Whirring and grinding sounds are coming from every window and door.

I have often wondered what goes on in there. Pa speaks of the mill and Mr. Birkett with admiration. Boy, would I love to see what is inside the big three story building. I wonder what all those machines I can see through the windows do. Perhaps Pa will ask if we can be taken on a tour. Golly, that would be really exciting. I have often wondered how our wheat is ground into such fine flour. Pa can't grind grain that fine with our windmill powered mill. That is why he only grinds feed for the livestock. Ma needs finely ground flour for baking bread, cookies and such.

"Pa, do you think we can see what goes on inside the mill?" I ask. Mary looks at me with surprise. I guess she hadn't thought of the possibility of seeing the interior of the massive building. The thought of going into the building with all its mysterious noises and strange looking machinery is a little unsettling.

"Perhaps," is all Pa says. He is smiling though. That is a good sign.

We will stop at the mill office after lunch to purchase one hundred and fifty pounds of wheat flour and one hundred pounds of cornmeal. These are for our needs and those of Aunt Liz and Uncle Jerome.

We cross the street and climb the six steps that lead to the office door. Once inside, we find ourselves with a young man who is seated at a small desk. He is using a chair that has large wheels so he can quickly move himself from his desk to a table across the small room. The wooden floor shows the marks of his many trips back and forth across the room. The desk and table are littered with many papers. Some are piled several inches high, others are stuck on long spikes that come through the wall next to his desk. Pa introduces him to us as Andy.

"Hello, Mr. Lee," says the young man as he stands. "Do you need some flour?"

"Yes, Andy. The Missus says we are about out." Pa places our order and Andy carefully writes it on a paper. "Your order will be ready for you in a few minutes," Andy says as he again rises from his terrific wheeled chair. "It will be on the loading dock for you anytime this afternoon."

"Thank you, Andy. Do you think the family could have a quick tour of the mill?" Pa asks. "We would be most interested. The children would like to know what happens to our wheat."

"I'll ask Mr. Birkett." Andy opens the door to the inner office and steps inside. Quietly closing the door behind him. In a moment he returns. "Mr. Birkett will take you himself," he announces and sits on his wheeled chair. "You may leave your picnic things here."

"Thank you, Andy," Pa says.

We step into the inner office and find Mr. Clarence Birkett sitting at a large roll top desk. He stands as we enter. I quickly glance around the room to satisfy my curiosity. This office is much more plush than that of Mr. William Fenton.

Oak file cabinets line one wall. I look at Mr. Birkett's big desk. It is made of oak too. Then I realize all the furniture is made of the same kind and color of wood. The place seems very fancy for a business office. On a table across the room, are samples of the mill's products. Boxes and bags are labeled First Prize Buckwheat Flour and Bessie Brand Pastry Flour.

Pa proudly introduces his family one by one beginning with Ma and ending with little Carolyn. Mr. Birkett says he will be pleased to take us on a tour of the mill. We children are most polite and I am thrilled to meet this famous businessman. He is a pillar of Penn Yan business having been a principal in the mill since 1887. He and his partner, Mr. Russell expanded the mill to its present size.

"Please watch your step when we are in the plant," Mr. Birkett instructs in a very deep and dignified voice. "This part of the building is old, having been built in 1824 and the stairs are steep and narrow."

Pa is carrying Carolyn on his shoulder and I have Mary by the hand. She whispers to me, "Do you think there are any mice or rats in here? I don't want to see them if there are."

Mr. Birkett laughs and says, "I heard your question, young lady. There are no rats or mice in this building. Not live ones anyway. Our night watchman spends a good deal of his time trapping them. Does that make you feel any better?"

"Yes, sir," Mary says gratefully. "Thank you." I give her hand a little squeeze. She is blushing from the attention paid to her by this famous man.

Mr. Birkett escorts us into a big room that has square wooden chutes in it. A fine dusting of flour is over everything. Overhead line shafts, belts and pulleys are running in many directions. Huge beams support the floor above. The complexity is beyond my comprehension. Above our heads is a large pulley system that changes the direction of power from horizontal to vertical. Whirring belts are everywhere.

"These," says Mr. Birkett as he points to the chutes, "move the flour that is being processed from one location to another." He opens a little door and we can look into a chute that is not in use. Inside is a belt with little cup like shelves on it every few inches. "These carry the partly milled flour for additional processing. They are called bucket elevators."

I must have looked puzzled because Mr. Birkett suddenly stops talking. "I must start at the beginning of the process. First the wheat grains are cleaned of foreign matter and graded by size. This is done by passing the wheat through tumbling sieves in an area we call the receiving pit. Air is also blown across the grain to help in the cleaning. Large fans are used for this purpose."

"Next comes a process called tempering. There are several ways of doing this but here we wet the grain to cause the bran or husk to swell so that it can easily be separated from the kernel. Sieves and air flow are used to make the separation. During this process, the central portion of the grain does not get wet. This part is nutritive and is ground to make flour. The purpose of tempering is to aid in removing the bran from the wheat kernel. It would not do to have bran mixed with the finished pastry flour. The bran is used in animal feed."

"Then, the kernels are ground using metal rollers with successively finer corrugations. It is elevated to the floor above by the bucket elevators and comes back down to the rollers to be ground again. Between each grinding the flour is put through ever finer sieves until all is ground to perfection. Bucket elevators carry the finished product to a storage area where it goes into bags or barrels. The Birkett Mills produces only the highest quality flour at a reasonable cost," says Mr. Birkett in a proud, business like voice.

"How long does this process take?" Ruthie asks.

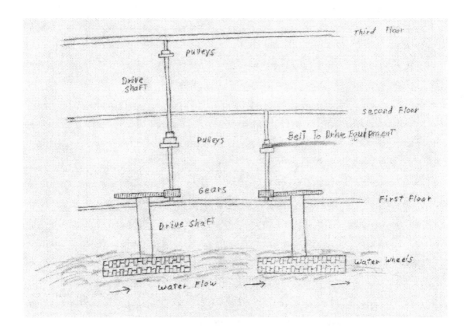

Mr. Birkett says, "The actual grinding takes about an hour but the tempering and cleaning add several more hours so it may take six hours from start to finished flour in the bag or barrel. Of course graham, or whole wheat flour is milled a little quicker as all the bran is not removed."

Then he points out two big round covered tubs on sturdy legs. "Inside these are mill stones that grind the buckwheat," shouts Mr. Birkett. "Over here is the set of sieves it passes through."

"Sir, why is buckwheat flour ground differently from wheat flour?" I ask.

"That is a good question, young man. The reason is that wheat is most usually ground into flour while buckwheat is most usually ground for cereal in this mill. Grinding for cereal is not as complex so there aren't as many steps necessary."

"Oh, I understand," I say thoughtfully.

Mr. Birkett must shout his explanations as it is even more noisy due to the rumble of large gears and whirr of belts and pulleys. Then we come to the start of all activity, the right front corner of the building.

"This part of the building is over a part of the Keuka Lake outlet channel," explains our guide. "Below the floor we are standing on are the two horizontal water wheels that power some of the machinery in the mill. In the early days they delivered power to the whole mill. Now, of course, we have much more equipment and use steam power too. The water wheels are made of cast iron and have been in use since the early 1880s."

Whirring directly in front of us are the two large vertical power shafts. They are rotating very rapidly as are the huge set of gears connected to each of them. Several large drive belts sprout from this area. This unit of machinery is housed inside a wooden fence for safety reasons.

The feeling of power is terrific. I am awed by it. I glance at Pa and see that little Carolyn is hiding her face in his shoulder. She has her fingers stuck in her ears. Pa looks as if he is enjoying the mighty power too. Ma is holding tight to his free arm but I think she is captivated by the marvelous energy in front of us.

Mary first looks at the rotating machinery and then at me. Her mouth is hanging open and her eyes are wide. I know I must look the same. I say, "Wow!" to her. She looks uneasy so I again take her hand to give her comfort. Mr. Birkett points to a slot in the floor where the huge cast-iron water wheels are visible below. Around them swirl the dark, rapidly moving water of the Keuka Lake outlet.

We return to the quiet of Mr. Birkett's office and he explains about the use of the water wheels.

"Children, I'm sure your teachers have explained to you the very long history of the use of flowing water and wind power to do useful work." We gravely nod our heads. Mr. Birkett continues with, "Mills were the first engines of civilization. The early Roman mills used waterpower to turn the mill stones. Why, only feet from here was located the sawmill that prepared the timbers and framing for the oldest parts of the first grist mill on the outlet. That was about one hundred years ago, he says proudly."

I feel a tingle go down my spine. Mr. Birkett's words are awe inspiring.

We stand quietly in the office. "Ahm, harumph," Mr. Birkett says. Then he blows his nose loudly. "You must excuse me now, work to do, you know." He sits at his big desk and begins to look at some papers. This is the signal our visit at the Birkett Mills is over. One by one the family waves good-bye to Andy as we walk through his office.

Together we walk to Hoban's livery to get the wagon and team. The horses nicker softly and prick their ears when they see Pa and me. I sure wish Sally would greet me that way when I walk up to her. I wonder if she ever will. We drive over to the mill loading dock and pick up the two barrels of flour and cornmeal. Pa pays Andy $2.40 for the wheat flour and $1.00 for the cornmeal. The barrels just fit into the back of the democrat wagon with the tailboard down. They are tied to the box of the wagon with a short rope. I hold the empty picnic basket on my lap and Mary has the milk can between her feet.

On our way out Elm Street, we turn into the lane that leads to the boat yard. Uncle Philo, Mr. Hackett, his engineer, and two Stone brothers, Howard and Alvin, his deckhands, are making the final preparations for launching the *Cricket*.

"Halloo in the *Cricket*," Pa calls loudly as we drive up.

"Halloo yourself," replies a smiling Uncle Philo. "I'll be right down." Uncle Philo scrambles down the ladder and walks to our wagon. "Are you coming to the launch tomorrow?" he asks eagerly. "I was going to stop by Henry's and your places tonight to ask for your help."

"Philo, you aren't going to launch on a Sunday?" Ma asks sharply.

"Yes I am, Ellen. It's the best time as there will be lots of people who will come and watch the excitement. It will get the steamboating season off to a rousing start. Will you be able to help with your teams and tackle, Charlie?"

"You bet, Philo. We wouldn't miss it for the world would we Danny? I'll get Henry and Jay to join us."

"No, Sir!" I say smartly. Perhaps I will be able to help handle a team or something else useful. I don't want to just be a bystander like last year. "Pa can I drive a team this year?" I ask hopefully.

"Well, I don't know. Let me think about it. Launching the *Cricket* is very dangerous work with four straining teams and tons of force on the tackle. I'll see if there is something you can do to help us."

"Thanks, Pa." I glance at Ma. She is looking sternly at Pa and Uncle Philo. I hope she doesn't tell Pa I am not to help. She will want me to go to Sunday School.

"What time do you want us here, Philo?"

"As soon after sunrise as you can. Launching is no job to be rushed. I'll have the Knapp House bring out some dinner for our noon meal."

"All right, you can count on us," Pa replies.

CHAPTER 7

▼

VISIT TO UNCLE JEROME AND AUNT LIZ

The rest of our trip home is uneventful. Ma is sitting on the back seat with Ruthie and Carolyn. She says not a word all the way home. Mary and I are sitting on the front seat with Pa. He lets me drive Andy and Toby when we are out of town. They trot along nicely though they have a heavy load to pull. I let them walk going up the steep parts of the Ridge Road.

When we arrive home, Pa says, "Danny, please take some of the flour and cornmeal down to Aunt Liz. If you don't stay too long, you can return before dark. Check the lake level and make sure they don't need our help to move their belongings. Ruth, please transfer the flour and meal to sacks for Danny."

"Yes, Pa," Ruthie says. "How much should I give them?"

"Oh, about twenty-five pounds of each."

"I will hang up your new suit for you," Mary says. "You wouldn't want to get it all wrinkles before you have even worn it."

"Thanks, Sis." I find two flour sacks for Ruthie.

"C'mon, Danny, you can hold the sacks open." Ruthie transfers the flour and cornmeal without spilling even a little bit. I know I could not have done that.

Pa tightly ties the bags shut with thin cord. He quietly says to me, "I'm worried about the lake level. Look and see if the water has reached the big willow tree in their front yard. If it is that high now, I think they are going to have bad trouble. We are not finished with the spring rains and the ground is saturated with water. There is no place for additional rain to go but directly into the lake."

"There isn't anything that can be done for them now are there?" I ask.

"No, except move their belongings to the second floor of their house and bring their livestock up here. If I know Uncle, he is not going to want to do that until he has to. He will want to hold out as long as possible thinking the water will go down. I hope he won't be too proud to ask for our help."

"All right, Pa, I'll check the lake level and see what Uncle Jerome and Aunt Liz have to say about the possibility of their house being flooded. I'll be back in time to do chores."

"Good boy."

Happily I saddle Sally while Pa ties the two bags of flour together with a short cord and places them across the old saddle. Down the bluff to Uncle Jerome and Aunt Liz's house on the shore of the lake we go. Sally seems to be glad to be outside and beautifully trots down the road. We slow to a walk where it is extra muddy so she will not slip and possibly fall.

I allow myself to think about using her to explore down the west side of the bluff and look for the place Captain Williamson's camp was located. What a swell time that will be. Just Sally and me. I'll pretend I'm a surveyor working with Captain Williamson. Perhaps I can explore next Saturday.

If I have all day, I will look for the Indian family too. Doc says there is an Indian family somewhere over by Branchport. I wonder why Pa hadn't mentioned them? They must be very different from us.

When I arrive at the edge of the lake, I find more than half of Uncle's front yard underwater. The small waves are almost lapping the big willow tree trunk. The lowest willow branches are touching the water. I have never seen Keuka Lake so high.

There still are some chunks of ice left from the piled up slabs scattered about. They have been frozen to the ground during a thaw and quick freeze. Most ice is gone having floated away in the high water and strong waves that come with spring winds. There are only about ten feet of almost level land between the house and water. If the lake comes up a few inches, the water will be at the house.

Uncle Jerome is in the barn when I arrive.

"Hello Uncle Jerome," I shout. I dismount and tie Sally to the hitching post.

"Why, hello Danny. How nice to see you. What are you doing here?" He stops putting away some old harness.

"Pa sent me down to see how the lake level is and to bring some flour. We went to town this morning."

"Oh, the lake looks like it has gone down a little. I think we will be all right."

I look at the lake with concern. "Do you really think so, Uncle? Looks mighty high to me."

"Was a bit higher. Has gone down a little. Is this your new horse, Danny?" Uncle asks when we walk out of the barn. "She sure is a beauty."

"Yes, this is Sally," I say as Uncle slides the bags of flour off the saddle. "She has a wonderful gait. Would you like to give her a try?"

"Don't mind if I do," says the old man. The mare shies away from Uncle when he tries to rub her forehead where her white stripe is.

"She is a little skittish, don't you think? How long have you had her?"

"Yes, but Pa thinks it is just because she doesn't know us. What do you think? We have had her about three weeks."

I want the mare to love me as I love her and hope Uncle will think she is a good horse. He is a good judge of horses and I know he will give an honest judgment. He puts the bags of flour on the porch.

"Well, that could be so. Hold her head while I lengthen the stirrup leathers. I'll take her for a little ride and let you know what I think. She sure is a good looker. What did you say her name is?"

"Sally, that is what Mr. Argyle called her so I kept the name. I like it, and I think it fits the horse, don't you?"

"Yes, I do. It's a right smart name for a smart looking horse."

I am pleased about Uncle's opinion of my mare.

Uncle mounts carefully and rides out the lane to the road. He disappears around the bend toward the Marshall place.

I go into the house to give the wheat flour and cornmeal to Aunt Liz.

"Land sakes, it is good to see you Danny," Aunt Liz exclaims. "How are all your folks? Please thank them for the supplies. It was kind of you to bring them down to us."

"You are welcome Aunt Liz. Pa wanted me to come and see how the lake level is." After I drag the two sacks into the kitchen and face Aunt Liz, I realize I am a little taller than she is. More proof I have, at last, begun to grow. I'm thrilled, two sizes larger suit and a bit taller than Aunt Liz. Progress at last!

"Yes, I will. Everyone is fine, Aunt Liz. How are you? Uncle looks well."

"Yes, we are both are in good health. The high water has me very worried though. We have never seen it so high."

"There isn't anything that can be done about it, is there? Uncle says it has gone down a little."

"Well, he would say that. I do not think it has gone down one bit. No sense of doing anything now. We just have to be ready to move all our belongings to the second floor of the house if it becomes necessary. Mr. Marshall and Mr. Simmons said they would give us a hand if need be. Jerome and I hope their help will not be required."

"I hope not too. Pa says to send us word if you need help. We will take in your livestock if need be. We were in town this morning and saw that the gate at the dam is wide open to let out as much water as is possible. I hope it does not rain a lot until the level is more normal."

"That's good to know," Aunt Liz says quickly. "If it doesn't rain much, we should be in good shape. Spring is often troublesome due to lots of rain but we had so much snow in January the danger of a flood is much greater. I try not to worry but it is difficult not to."

"Help yourself to some johnny cake. Just baked it this morning. There are honey and molasses on the shelf."

"What did you do while you were in town?" Aunt Liz asks.

"We went shopping for a suit for me and shoes for the girls for Easter. Ma got some fabric to make a new dress. Mr. Birkett took us on a tour of the mills. That was very interesting as I had no idea what goes on inside a merchant mill. Pa found out the name of the man who is interested in buying the Wagener place from Grandpa Scott."

"Is that so? What is his name? Is it anyone we know?" Aunt Liz asks.

"No, he is from out of town. His name is Mr. Overhouser."

"Oh, well, that is interesting, Danny, you might have a new neighbor."

"Yes, I hope he has a son I can play with if he buys the place. Thanks for the johnny cake, Aunt Liz." I give her a little hug.

I spread butter on a thick slab of johnny cake and carefully drizzle on some golden honey. Aunt Liz pours a steaming cup of tea and places my treat in the oven of her cook stove for a few minutes to melt the butter. Yum! There is nothing better than melted butter, honey and warm johnny cake.

I am watching out the kitchen window for the return of Uncle Jerome and Sally. Soon Uncle comes riding along the lane. He has a big grin on his face. Even from this distance I see a sparkle in his pale blue eyes. He likes Sally. I run out to see what he has to say about her.

"You have a humdinger of a horse here, Danny."

"Gee thanks, Uncle. She is very well behaved. I love her but she doesn't seem to like me." I hold Sally's bridle while Uncle dismounts.

"Why, how do you mean?"

"Well, she doesn't greet me like Bess and the other horses do. I feel she doesn't want to be with me."

"Now just a minute," he says sharply. "You don't really expect this horse to take to you right away do you? She has a lot to learn. Horses have feelings too, you know. Her life has changed and she wonders what has happened. She probably misses her master, old horse pals and her stall. You haven't had her long enough for her to be comfortable with you yet. Give her time."

"Oh, yes, Uncle Jerome. I understand now. I wasn't thinking about her that way. Sally would be upset and confused. I hope she will feel more comfortable and like me and her new home soon."

"I'm sure she will," says Uncle with a warm smile and a friendly pat for Sally. "Just treat her kindly, which I know you will do, and she will come around soon. A carrot or two will help also."

"I had best be on my way," I say. "Chores to do you know." Uncle adjusts the stirrup leathers for me and helps me mount my horse. I wave good-bye to Aunt Liz who is standing on the kitchen porch.

"Good bye, Uncle. Remember to send us word if you need any help."

"Yes, I will. Have a nice ride home."

As Sally trots down the lane, I turn to wave to Uncle Jerome. He is already walking toward his house. I can see he is looking at the lake and shaking his head. He talked as if he had no concern but now I know he does.

I wonder what it would be like to have Keuka Lake water flowing into the basement and the first floor of your house. I have heard of people having flood damage from a stream overflowing its banks but never from the lake. Golly, I hope it doesn't happen.

How would the water be gotten out of the basement after the lake level went down? Some kind of pump would have to be used, I suppose. Uncle's house isn't the only one along the lake that is close to the water. Others may be closer and may be flooded already. What an interesting thing to think about. I'll bet the high water is a problem for some folks. Their place would be badly damaged by water.

When I arrive home, I find Pa and Doc working on rebuilding our sledge. They are reinforcing the platform the men stand on for driving fence posts and posts in the vineyards. This sledge is not pulled on snow but is used on the ground. It must be strong and heavily built for a man to stand on and use an eight or ten pound maul to drive the posts into the ground.

Under the upright part, will be a pile of new posts. Any broken posts will be taken to the house to be cut up for firewood. The new posts had been split from locust tree logs last month. They are six feet long with a pointed end for driving into the still frozen ground. An axe was used to sharpen the stakes.

The sledge will be pulled through the vineyards. Each post will be checked to make sure it is solid in the ground. Any missing staples that hold the wires will be replaced. The man standing on the platform would drive a new post into the ground with his maul and give each old post a wack or two to make sure they are solid.

Another vineyard job at this time is to tighten any sagging wires so they will give good support to the growing vines.

"Hello, Danny. What is the lake level like?" Pa asks as he puts down his hammer. Doc looks up from his work of sawing across a thick six inch oak plank.

"It is nearly up to Uncle Jerome's willow tree," I say. "He thinks they will be all right if it doesn't rain for the next few days. But I think he is very worried."

"Not much chance of that this time of the year," Doc says as he takes off his hat and rubs his forehead.

"Does he have anything he wants us to do for him now?" Pa asks. "We will just have to hope for dry weather."

"No, he said Mr. Marshall and Mr. Simons offered to help move their belongings if need be. I told him to be sure to send for us if he wants to move."

"That's good. With all of us working, it won't take long to move their belongings out of harm's way. Perhaps they won't be flooded but it sure doesn't look good right now."

I put Sally away and do the rest of my evening chores.

At the supper table, Mary and Carolyn are quiet and sad. I know they feel the absence of Miss Spaulding. So does Uncle Ed. He has been moping around something awful.

CHAPTER 8

▼

THE LAUNCH OF
THE CRICKET

We get up early Sunday morning to do our chores before riding to the boat yard to help Uncle Philo.

Before breakfast, I find Mary all alone in the parlor. She has her Sunday School dress on and is sitting on the horse hair sofa with her legs dangling. I can see that the usually perky Mary is unhappy. She is pouting and rapidly swinging her legs.

"What is wrong?" I ask.

"I wish I could go to the launch of the *Cricket* with you and the men," she says sadly. "I don't get to do anything interesting or exciting because I am a girl. It just isn't fair."

"Have you asked Ma if you can go with us?"

"Of course I asked," Mary answers sharply. She looks up at me with angry eyes.

Guess it was a stupid question.

"Well, exactly what did she say?"

"She said it is unseemly for a girl to be interested in such things. I don't even know what unseemly means."

"It means inappropriate, Mary," Ruthie explains as she comes into the room.

"Well, it really isn't an interest for a girl you know," I say quickly. I instantly regret having said that. Mary looks at me with an icy stare.

"You needn't be so smug, smarty pants Danny," Ruthie says quickly. "Ma doesn't want you to go with the men either. She said it is too dangerous and that you should go to Sunday School. She said you need the influence of Sunday School and not that of your cousin Jay."

"Oh, oh, when did she say that?" I ask, concerned I will not be able to go on my big adventure.

"Oh, a little while ago."

"What did Pa say?"

"He said you would be needed as a helper. Then Uncle Philo won't need to hire an extra man. But it sounded like you aren't going to be allowed to do much."

"Oh, no. That's not going to be any fun. I want a part just like the men do."

"Perhaps you will not even be going," Ruthie says in a taunting voice. "A little twerp like you would just be in the way."

"I'll see about that," I call as I run from the room. Being stuck home with the girls, won't be fun on such a nice day. I'll hunt up Pa and see what he has to say. He has to let me help launch Uncle Philo's big boat.

I know where the men will be, in the tool shed getting our screw jacks and block and tackle together. They will be checking the strong ropes to make sure there aren't any frayed spots. It would be a very dangerous situation to have a rope break while under heavy tension. The suddenly freed ends would go flying and might strike someone or a team of horses. The team might even stumble and fall if suddenly released from their great effort.

Even four teams of draft horses will not be strong enough to move the *Cricket* into the water without the help of mechanics. Uncle Henry will bring his screw jacks and block and tackle too. I know they will need this equipment from listening to the men talk last fall when they hauled the boat out of the water for the winter.

Uncle Henry is two years younger than my Pa and looks a lot like him but is not quite as tall. He also has a short black beard and dark eyes. Pa is clean shaven and has blue eyes like mine.

Moving the large steamboats into and out of the water requires much help. Uncle Philo only has to hire one team from Mr. Hoban's livery. The other three teams will be lent to him by Pa and Uncle Henry. In return our family will receive free boat rides on the *Cricket* and the *Earl*.

Just as I figured, Pa and Uncle Ed are in the tool shed. Bess and Kit are hitched to our hay wagon and the men are loading heavy steel levers, screw jacks and the block and tackle onto the wagon. There are also lengths of heavy chain, large clevis shackles, and two big coils of very strong rope. Pa's eight pound and ten pound mauls are put on the wagon too. Bess and Kit have on their heaviest harness with extra padding under the collars.

Think positively I say to myself, "Good morning Pa, good morning, Uncle Ed. Can I be of help getting the tools ready?"

"No, thanks, Danny. We are almost finished here. These things are too heavy for you anyway."

"I can get these shackles for you," I say. It takes both hands and I still can carry only one at a time.

"Will I be driving one of our teams when it is time to haul the boat into the water?" I ask hopefully.

"Yes, that is the plan, Danny." Pa is looking at me sharply. "You can't do the heavy work so handling Bess and Kit are the only thing you can do. You aren't to do anything under the boat or even near to the boat. Is that understood? Once we get the equipment in place, you will drive this team and you will stay clear of the boat. Agreed?"

"Yes, sir!" Positive thinking worked. I will be a big part of the launch of the *Cricket*. I will do a man's job. "Thank you for letting me help."

"It is not going to be a lark you know. You must pay attention to what you are doing and do precisely what you are told and when you are told it. A mistake could get someone badly hurt. Get your heavy leather gloves. We are about ready to start for town."

"Yes sir, Pa." Yahoo! I say to myself. I'm going to be a help after all.

Doc joins us with Jim and Dan who are tied to the back of the hay wagon by their leads. They have on their heaviest harness too. Soon we are on our way.

The road is very rutty and there are still large mud puddles for the horses to splash through. I must hold on hard to the edge of the wagon to keep from falling off.

We meet Uncle Henry and Cousin Jay who are waiting for us where their lane meets the Ridge Road. They have their team of Percheron draft horses. This breed of draft horse was developed in France. They are slightly smaller than our Belgian horses and are a little faster on their feet. Their power is not quite as great as that of Belgian horses but they can do plenty of hard work.

Uncle Henry's team is mostly black. One, named Blaze, has a white area on his right hind leg and a white blaze on his face. The other horse is named Blackie and is all black. Our horses are the reddish blond of the Belgian draft horse with light colored mane, tail and lower legs.

Uncle Henry's equipment is placed on our hay wagon and Blaze and Blackie are tied behind Jim and Dan.

We meet several Bluff Point neighbor families who wave and smile as we drive by. The equipment we have with us and the time of year tells them where we are going and why.

Uncle Philo is famous as a steamboat captain and part owner of the Lee Line of boats. Uncle Philo is five years younger than my Pa. He has a full black beard and light blue eyes. He is taller and bigger than Pa. He may look stern but we know he is full of fun and adventure.

Jay and I sit on the tailboard of the wagon and watch the horses behind us. The jingling harness play a jolly tune. Their huge feet make a powerful beat but their nice clean legs and bellies are soon splattered with mud from the sloppy road.

We rumble, bump, and crash our way over the ruts in the dry places and even the wagon becomes splattered with muck in the wet spots.

The boat yard is already full of activity when we drive in. Uncle Philo greets us with a broad smile and a wave. He is dressed in a blue denim shirt, muddy work boots, and overalls. It sure is strange to see him without his captain's outfit. With him are Mr. Hackett, and the two Stone brothers. They are dressed in heavy work clothes too.

"Thank you for coming, Charlie and Henry," Uncle Philo calls. "I see you have brought good help with you. Hello, Doc hello Ed. Hello, boys."

"Yes-sir-ree," Pa says with a sparkle in his eye. "Jay and Danny can handle the teams as well as any of us." And Doc will keep all of us out of trouble. With this remark, Pa gives Doc a kindly pat on the shoulder. Doc is grinning with pleasure. He knows his knowledge and experience is always appreciated.

Mr. Hackett is a very tall and very large black man. He knows as much about steam engines and other machinery as does Uncle Philo. He is also very strong. Mr. Hackett has been the engineer on the *Cricket* since the boat was built early in 1894. He oversaw the instillation of the engines.

I spoke with him a lot when I rode on the steamboat last summer. He showed me all about the steam engines on Uncle's boat. He likes me to ask him questions about the *Cricket* and his life before he and his family came to Penn Yan. Mr. Hackett is the same age as Doc, sixty-six.

Mr. Hackett escaped from slavery in the state of Georgia in 1858. He told me he did this by hiding in a barrel and having it shipped north. He was in the large barrel for five days on the train.

His travels were known to members of the Underground Railroad. They would meet the train when it stopped at night to let him out and give him food and water. Finally he was delivered to Elmira in the southern part of New York state. People there, who were part of the underground railroad, learned he knew a lot about steam engines and sent him onto Penn Yan where steamboats were being used on Keuka Lake as well as other nearby lakes.

The folks who helped Mr. Hackett in Elmira were sure he would find a good job because of his knowledge of steam engines. The man he worked for in Georgia owned several stationary steam engines and Mr. Hackett was in charge of them. These engines were used to power a sawmill, gristmill, and a cotton gin. He quickly found a job as engineer on a steamboat on Keuka Lake and later came to work for my uncle.

Mr. Hackett also told me he fought in the Civil War. He was in Company I of the 16th United States Colored Troops. His first name is William but all we children call him Mr. Hackett. The men call him Hack. He lives on Jackson Street in Penn Yan with his wife Maria and son Fred.

Company I of the 16th United States Colored Troops was involved in the Battle of Nashville December fifteenth and sixteenth of 1864. They were in pursuit of Confederate Major General Hood to the Tennessee River, for the following twelve days. Mr. Hackett has promised to tell me about the Battle of Nashville sometime.

The Stone brothers are small men. Wiry Ma calls them. They have worked for Uncle Philo since the *Cricket* was first launched also. Howard Stone is twelve years younger than Uncle Philo. Alvin Stone is eleven years younger than Uncle Philo.

The Stone brothers were born at Fish Creek in Oneida County. Their family came to live in Branchport when they were two and one year old. Growing up there, they were fascinated by the steamboats plying the beautiful waters of Keuka Lake. Steamboating was in their blood as their father, the senior Alvin Stone had worked on steamboats on Oneida Lake. The Philo Lee and senior Alvin Stone families live near each other in Branchport and that is how the Stone brothers became deck hands for the Lee Line of steamboats.

We children have been given permission to call the Stone brothers Mr. Howard and Mr. Alvin.

"All right, lets get started," Uncle Philo says. He is all business when it comes to steamboating. "You boys tend to the teams and then lay out the shackles, rope and tackle."

"We will begin the job of taking the boat off the blocks and getting it onto the rollers. You boys stay away from the boat. We don't want to worry about you getting hurt or being in the way. Removing the blocks is heavy and very difficult work. And don't lift those lengths of chain. They are too heavy for you."

"Aw, we can handle the chain," protests Jay.

"No, I don't want you to struggle with them. Do what you are told, Jay. You do remember how the tackle is set up from last year, don't you?"

"Yes, Uncle Philo. I can do it." Jay is two years older than I and likes to show off his abilities to me.

"Good, show Danny so he can learn too. Understanding the mechanics of block and tackle is a very useful thing to know. I will ring the boat's bell when we are ready for you."

Jay and I say, "Yes, sir," and begin our work by bringing buckets of water to the horses. Uncle Philo hired a team of Clydesdales from Mr. Hoban.

"Jay, aren't these horses beautiful?" I exclaim. "They are larger than Big Jim and Big Dan." I give each of them a pat on the neck and a rub on their white forehead. They are a darker chestnut color than our Belgians and are a little taller. Their mane and tail are a dark brown. The lower leg is white with lots more fur than our teams. Their hooves are huge.

"Yes, I would like to have a team just like them when I have my own farm."

"I wonder who is going to drive them?" I ask.

"Mr. Alvin did last fall when they took the boat out of the water. Mr. Alvin, Doc, you and I will handle the teams while my Pa, your Pa, Uncle Ed and Mr. Howard keep the rollers properly placed under the boat cradle."

"What are they doing now?" I ask.

"They are replacing the blocks with the rollers," says Jay. He looks at me as if I should not have needed to ask. "The rollers are placed on either side of the keel."

"Oh, I get it. They jack the boat up with the screw jacks, take out the blocks one by one and lay down log rollers in their place. They are using the mauls to drive out the blocks."

"Yes, that is right. But it is much easier said than done," Jay says. "The boat will be rolled into the water on the log rollers. The men will then have to pull the rollers out of the water and the boat will be floating free."

"Wow, a big job," I blurt out. "Wait a minute, what will Uncle Philo and Mr. Hackett be doing?"

"Yes it sure is. Uncle Philo will direct the whole process from the deck of the boat where he can see all that is going on. He and Mr. Hackett will change the position of the tackle on the boat as it moves into the water. They will carefully watch and make sure nothing is going wrong."

We finish watering the teams and then carefully lay out the block and tackle. The tackle must not become kinked or tangled. Uncle Philo brought his two sets of tackle and we lay these out too. Jay shows me where they go and how the parts are placed. They are too heavy and large for us to carry alone so we each take an end and drag them between us. Jay knows just where to place each part as he helped last fall. I wasn't allowed to help then.

When we have finished, Jay and I wander around looking at the nearby boats and watch the men working to get them ready to launch.

The boat yard is a busy place this time of year. In a few weeks it will be empty of boats as they all will be in use on the lake. Some carry just passengers and small freight like the *Earl* which is also managed by Uncle Philo. Others like the *Cricket* carry passengers and large freight such as produce at harvest time. Some families have their own steam launches for personal transportation. There are some steam barges on the lake that just carry freight such as livestock or produce.

CLANG, CLANG, CLANG, CLANG! "Come on, they're ready for us," Jay shouts.

"Oh boy," I exclaim. We run top speed back to the boat and arrive just in time to see Mr. Hackett being rowed by Mr. Howard out to the pilings set in the bottom of the channel about twenty feet from shore.

The clevis shackles will be used to attach the chains to the pilings. Each set of pulleys is called a block. The rope is the tackle. The fixed block is attached to the chain with another clevis shackle. The moving block is attached to the boat cleats and is what slowly moves the boat.

The teams of horses pull on the free end of the rope. There are two pulleys on the moving and two pulleys on the fixed end of this set of tackle. This way the pulling force of the teams will be increased by four times. Once in the water, the boat will be moored to the pilings.

"All right, boys, it's time for you to go to work," Uncle Henry says. "Jay, do you remember where the teams are placed?"

"Yes, Pa, I do."

"Good, get to it then. Please bring over the Clydesdales too."

First we drive the two Belgian teams and place them side by side on the left or port side of the steamboat. Then Jay and I drive the Puncheon and Clydesdale teams into place on the right or starboard side. This way the power of the teams will be balanced on each side of the boat.

Left and right sides of a boat are determined when facing the front or bow. The back of a boat is called the stern.

Uncle Philo and Mr. Hackett are attaching the moving ends of the block and tackle to the bow cleats of the *Cricket*.

Finally all is ready. A great crowd of onlookers has gathered. Some have brought their picnic lunch and are sitting on blankets eating and watching. This is the second year for the *Cricket*. She is Penn Yan's newest steamboat and the townspeople want to be among the first to have a ride this season.

Uncle Philo is standing at the bow of his boat with his hand on the clapper for the boat's bell.

Doc, who will drive Jim and Dan, says to me, "When your uncle rings the bell we will drive our teams forward. The effort will be hard for them. We must urge them to keep a steady pull and to slowly move forward."

"I understand," I say eagerly. I don't see Pa or the other men. Then Pa and Uncle Henry come around the stern of the boat carrying a big roller between them.

"Are Uncle Ed and Mr. Howard on the other side of the boat with a roller?" I ask Doc.

"Right you are," Doc says.

CLANG!

"Giddap you horses!" shouts Doc as he flicks the reins on the backs of Jim and Dan.

"Giddap, Bess and Kit!" I shout in my best manly voice.

The horses surge ahead for a few seconds until the tackle is tight. Then they begin to strain in their harness. I can hear the leather creaking and see the great muscles bulging on the legs, chest, and rumps of the teams. Slowly they move ahead. "Good girl Bess, good girl Kit," I call. Their bodies are hunched down with the effort they must make. Slowly, ever so slowly they move ahead and slowly, ever so slowly the *Cricket* is pulled toward the rapidly moving water of the Keuka Lake outlet.

I make a quick glance at the boat just in time to see Pa and Uncle Henry place their roller under the bow of the boat.

We urge the horses to continue making their great effort. The bow of the steamboat is in the water. The great horses are breathing hard now and sweat is beginning to show on their bodies. I hope their effort is almost over. It has been going on for only a few minutes but it seems like forever. I risk another quick glance at the boat. It is more than half way into the water. Pa and Uncle Henry are fishing a roller out of the water. The bow of the boat is in the water and the horses are not making as much effort to move the boat. We continue a few more minutes and then....

CLANG, CLANG!

"That is the signal for us to stop," Doc shouts. "Your Uncle Philo needs to move the block and tackle."

"Whoa," Doc says. "Take a breather."

I can hear Mr. Alvin and Jay saying the same thing to the other two teams. "Whoa, Bess. Whoa, Kit," I shout. The horses seem glad to rest. They are standing with their heads down and their sides heaving. Their nostrils are wide open as they take in as much air as possible.

"I don't understand," I say. "What's going on? I can't see what Uncle Ed and Mr. Howard are doing."

"Look," Doc points. "The moving end of the tackle is even with the pilings. The teams have pulled the boat as far as they can for now. We will drive the teams to the starting place while your uncle and Mr. Hackett reattach the moving end of the tackle to the cleats midway down the side of the boat. Quickly remove the rope from the hitch so they will have the slack rope they need."

I do as I am told and watch Uncle Philo and Mr. Hackett adjust the tackle. Then the teams are returned to their starting point. The team's breathing has returned to normal by the time we hear another....

CLANG!

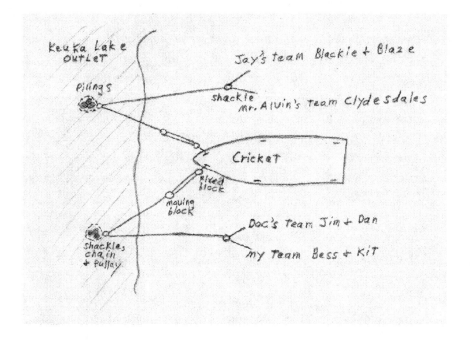

Again we urge the teams into motion and the boat slowly inches into the water of the outlet channel. The effort for the horses is easier now as some of the boat's length is supported by the water. Pa, Mr. Howard and Uncle Ed are pulling the last pair of rollers out of the water.

Shortly there are two clangs and we stop. "What should we do now?" I ask of Doc.

"As we want the *Cricket* to be bow into the current, and heading toward the lake, the boat will have to be turned by Mr. Alvin's and Jay's teams. Their tackle will be returned to the starboard bow cleat but not attached to the piling. Ours will be moved to the port stern cleat so we can help turn the boat too. Ours will still be attached to the piling so the stern will be pulled out into the water."

"Oh, I get it. Then Uncle Philo can cast lines to the pilings to hold the boat in place."

"Right as two rabbits," Doc says with a big grin. "The men will go onto the boat and start a fire in the boiler to begin to make steam."

"Will the boat be ready to use this afternoon?" I ask in surprise.

"Oh yes, indeed." Doc says, still grinning. "But first we get to eat dinner. We will have a grand feed."

I turn to look where he is looking and see the arrival of the delivery wagon from the Knapp House. Oh, good, I'm starving. Right away the wagon driver starts a small cooking fire in a stone fireplace. The cook is selecting pots and pans from the back of the wagon. I wonder what he is going to make?

There is no more time to think of food. We again give Uncle Philo slack line and back our teams. Mr. Alvin and Jay do the same. A single clang and we direct our teams ahead. I keep glancing behind me to watch the *Cricket* slowly turn. I see Pa and Uncle Henry clamber onto the boat and get ready with stern lines. Two clangs and we stop our teams.

A cry of approval and applause rises from the crowd of onlookers. I hope we have made a difficult job look easy. The Stone brothers climb onto the boat as Pa gets off. Soon smoke begins to pour from the smoke stack.

"Good work, Danny, you too, Doc," Pa calls as he walks to us. "When steam is up, we can go for a ride. Lets gather our tackle and that of Henry. Then we will eat dinner." I see Uncle Henry give Jay a big pat on the back. They have big grins on their faces. It is good to know your efforts are appreciated.

Doc says, "All went smoothly for us. You didn't have any trouble under the boat, did you?"

"No, not really. Removing the blocks was a little difficult and the rollers were hard to pull out of the channel. It would be good if we had a horse to help with that."

"We will have to remember to try that this fall. A horse to help move the rollers," Doc says thoughtfully.

Jay and I give the teams some hay, a measure of oats and pails of water for their dinner. They had worked the hardest of us all.

Then we join the men and sit under a nearby willow tree to eat our delicious noon meal served to us by a cook from the Knapp House. Yum, thick hot roast beef sandwiches, baked beans and fried potatoes, cold fried chicken and sweet pickles really hit the spot. Thick wedges of apple pie with cheese on top and steaming cups of coffee are for desert.

Mr. Hackett and the Stone brothers don't stay with us very long. The boiler must be fed enough coal to develop sufficient steam pressure to power the boat. It is their job to make sure the *Cricket* is ready for its first trip of 1895. They wolf down their food and take a slice of pie and a mug of coffee with them. Soon Uncle Philo joins them, pie in one hand and coffee in the other.

Pa, Uncle Henry and Uncle Ed know they have a few moments to relax before it will be time to help get the *Cricket* under way for its first cruise of the season.

CHAPTER 9

▼

STEAMBOATING

A stream of people file onto the *Cricket*. Uncle Philo, now dressed in his spiffy captain's outfit, is standing at the gangplank collecting the fare of ten cents.

Cousin Jay and I wait until the line ends. Then we start up the gangplank. "Take seats anywhere, boys," Uncle Philo says in his best captain's voice as we cross from land to boat. "Your good help is greatly appreciated."

"You are welcome, Uncle," we reply. We run up the steep stairs to the upper deck and seat ourselves in the bow just forward of the pilot-house. There are only straight backed wooden chairs here but we don't mind. The view of the lake is the best from the bow. From this spot I can pretend I am the pilot of the *Cricket*, skillfully directing her every move.

"Hey, Jay, do you ever wish you were the pilot or captain of a steam-boat?" I ask quietly. I hope he doesn't laugh at me for asking this.

"You bet I do. I wouldn't handle the boat the way Uncle does though. I'd race the other boats every chance I got. Would get more fares that way and add some excitement to steamboating."

"I think there are plenty of riders for all the boats and there is the freight too," I say. "It seems to me there is enough business so there is no need for tricks. My Ma says trying to outdo another boat captain can sometimes get out of hand."

"There you go being a goodie two shoes again. Don't you understand competition?" Jay laughs.

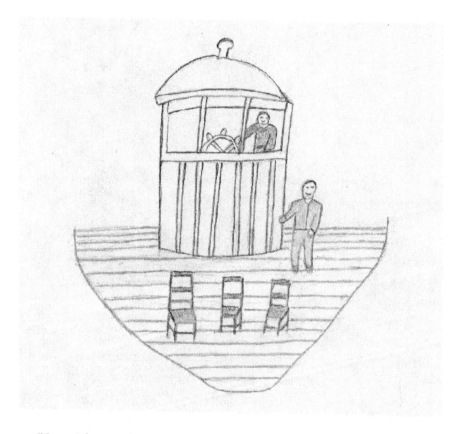

"Sure I know about competition. I don't like the boat captains to fight over riders or loads of freight though. Racing is dangerous too. Could blow up a boiler or have a collision."

"Ha, ha," laughs Jay. "You sure are a sissy. Don't you remember last year when the *Mary Belle* and the *Holmes* almost collided? It sure made exciting talk for quite a while. Nobody blows up a modern boiler. There are laws to prevent allowing too much pressure."

"I remember all right. I'm glad I wasn't on either of the boats. If you think a law is going to stop someone from allowing the build up of too much steam pressure you are naive," I say somewhat sharply.

Jay looks a little surprised with this remark. "I wish I had been on one of the boats that almost collided. It would have been exciting," he says with a gleam in his eye. "I suppose someone could get careless and blow up a boat. All it would take would be to wire the safety valve closed."

"Yes, that is right. Then a boiler explosion could occur," I reply.

I almost jump out of my skin when Uncle Philo blows one long blast on the boat steam whistle by pulling on a line in the pilothouse. This signals to everyone within earshot the boat is getting underway. The whistle is just behind us on top of the pilothouse. Mr. Alvin and Uncle Henry pull in the gangplank. Pa and Uncle Ed cast off the bow and stern lines and we begin to move ahead slowly.

Our first steamboat ride of the season has begun. There are many more to come as we will be using the boats for much of our transportation needs during the spring, summer and fall. I'll get to help as a deck hand during the summer when there is lots of excursion traffic. People even come from cities for a ride on Keuka Lake during a fine summer day or night.

Dark black smoke billows from the smoke stack as Mr. Hackett continues to build up steam in the boiler. We move at a slow speed in the narrow channel until we reach the open water of Keuka Lake. Then Uncle calls to Mr. Hackett for full throttle and the *Cricket* leaps ahead. How magnificent steam power is. Just riding on the *Cricket* is exciting for me. I don't need any near collisions.

Here, on the bow of the top deck the only sound to be heard is the swish of the bow cutting through the blue water far below us. I love to watch the sparkle of the sunlight on the bow wave as the boat glides ahead.

The lady and gentlemen passengers wrap their coats tightly about them and hold on their hats as it is windy and cold. Smiles of pleasure come over their faces for the joy of riding on the lake even if it is cold. The thermometer outside the pilothouse reads forty-five degrees. Only the most hardy sit on the open upper deck. A few are sitting behind the pilot house which protects them from the wind caused by the moving boat.

There are wooden benches with blue cushions on them and wicker chairs and rockers with blue and white flowered cushions for folks to sit on. A dark blue canvas canopy is over the deck behind the pilot house. Most everyone is inside the enclosed lower deck cabin where they are out of the wind and are warmed by heat from the boiler.

Some people are dressed in their Sunday best. Their children are sitting quietly by their parents' side. I recognize some of the town children from last year's rides on the *Cricket* or *Earl*. Jay and I wave our greetings. The boys are eager to move around the boat and ask permission of their parents to join Jay and me at the bow. Soon we have our own little group. The girls are left looking like little ladies sitting next to their mothers. I wonder if any of them secretly wish they could join the boys at the bow.

I don't want Uncle Philo to tell us not lean over the rail so I remind the boys myself. I know he is watching us from the pilothouse windows. A fall from the boat would be bad enough but a fall from the bow would mean being run over by the huge boat and sure death.

Now that we are on the lake, Uncle Philo directs the boat toward the west shore. He is hoping to find more people who want their first steamboat ride of the season. Our presence on the lake is visible for miles. Jay and I look ahead to see a group of people standing on the pier at Struble's Landing. One of the men is waving a red flag. He is signaling they want a ride.

Mr. Clinton Struble is a famous lawyer and businessman in Penn Yan. He has a large house in town on Main Street and a summer cottage at this steamboat landing. Mr. Struble is standing on the dock with his wife and two other people.

We watch in amazement and pride as our Uncle heads the big boat directly toward the end of the pier. Mr. Hackett has reduced our speed by closing the throttles on the steam engines. Then, at the last possible moment, Uncle sharply turns the boat to port, and we glide to a stop across the end of the pier and only a few feet away from it.

Mr. Alvin and Pa slide the shore end of the gangplank onto the pier and the passengers step aboard. Mr. Alvin collects the fare and returns the gangplank to the deck of the boat as Mr. Hackett opens the throttles. The *Cricket* rapidly picks up speed as Uncle Philo steers the boat out into the lake. Everything goes like clockwork. The boat is only stopped for a few minutes. When regular passenger service begins, there will be schedules to meet. No time will be wasted stopped at a pier.

"Wow, that is a jim-dandy way your uncle handles the boat at the dock. I wonder how he learned to do it?" asks one of the boys from town.

Jay and I laugh, "We have asked him and all he says is, 'Practice boys, practice'."

"I can do it when I'm rowing," Jay says proudly.

"Oh, yah that's nothing when you are in a little row boat," the town boy laughs.

"Oh, you don't even know how to row well," says another boy and gives him a friendly poke. "You keep going around in circles." We all laugh. Rowing a boat is learned early by children who live near the lake.

"I'll do better this year," says the boy with determination. "Just you wait and see."

"Say, you and Jay did a terrific job helping launch the boat into the channel," another boy says to me. "Our family brought a picnic lunch and watched you work. You sure are handy with those teams."

"It was great fun to be part of such a big job. My Pa has been letting me do lots of great things on our farm this year. I even have my own riding horse now," I say with pride.

"You do!" Jay exclaims. He has a look of hurt surprise on his face.

"Yah. Pa took her in payment for some oats and hay from Mr. Argyle."

"Oh, I didn't know. You lucky stiff. I don't have a horse of my own," says Jay whose face has hardened in anger.

"Yes, but you can ride Nick or Nack whenever you wish. I can't ride Andy or Toby."

"That's true," Jay says with a smile. "I'm a much better rider than you," he boasts. "You are too small and too weak to handle those spirited horses."

"You needn't keep reminding me, cousin," I say sharply. "I did ride Andy once when Pa was hurt by the cougar. That doesn't count though as Wild Andy was very tired from running all the way home after he escaped from the big cat. It's a good thing he didn't act up when I was on him because he would have thrown me for sure."

One of the younger boys is looking at me with admiration. I try to stand taller. It is nice to have an accomplishment to talk about.

The boat is directed along the west side of the east branch of the lake and makes another stop. This time it is at the Keuka College landing. Again Uncle expertly brings the *Cricket* to a stop across the end of the large dock. Here we pick up about ten more passengers. Most are college students. Dr. Ball, president of the college, is with the students. He looks around at the other passengers and I see a glimmer of recognition as his eyes meet mine. He smiles and offers a little wave. I wave back and watch as he sedately walks into the cabin.

Suddenly one of the town boys is hitting me in the ribs. "Do you know that old guy?" he asks loudly.

"Yes, I spoke with him once," I say proudly. "My Pa does business with him sometimes and he introduced me to Dr. Ball in his office at the college."

"Well, la-de-da," the town boy exclaims. "Ain't you grand. I wouldn't want that old guy talking to me."

"Why not? He is a nice man," I say quickly. I am surprised by this response to my knowing Dr. Ball.

"He's a fancy guy with some high-toned education. I don't want anything to do with anyone like that."

"He is a man with lots of book learning that's true but he is nice to me. I like him."

"Ha!" scoffs the boy from town. "You're as strange as he is," and walks away with his friends. It is like they don't want to be around me. I can hear them laughing as they move away from us.

"That was a dumb move, Danny," says Jay. "Don't you know you're not supposed to admit you like an educated person?"

"Well, I do like Dr. Ball and I don't care if the boys from town know it or not."

"They're going to laugh every time they see you," Jay warns.

"Let them laugh," I say loudly. I feel the heat of anger that comes with failure to understand why someone does or says something. I don't see anything wrong with talking with educated people. I might learn useful and interesting things from Dr. Ball.

By this time we have a full head of steam and the *Cricket* is moving at top speed. I look into the pilothouse and see Uncle Philo using a spyglass to see if there are any passengers ahead. I don't see any and say to Jay, "Let's go talk to Mr. Hackett and warm up. I'm getting cold standing out here in all this wind."

"Good idea, maybe he will let us shovel coal into the firebox of the boiler," says Jay with a grin.

We open the hatch that covers a route to the engine room. Carefully we climb down the little ladder.

"Hello boys," hollers Mr. Howard Stone. He is helping Mr. Hackett stoke the boiler. "Have you come to help shovel? Your uncle keeps asking for more speed. There isn't another boat up there to race is there?" he asks with a laugh.

"No, we are the only steamer out here. He just wants to go fast," replies Jay. "You know how he loves speed. Is there anything we can do to help you?"

"Yes, there is," Mr. Hackett says. "Check all the oil and grease cups to make sure they have lots in them. The links may be using more lubrication seeing this is the first time out this year."

"We can do that. That's an easy job. Come on, Danny." We work along each side of the powerful engines and examine the oil reservoirs and grease cups. They are all nearly full. "They're in good shape, Mr. Hackett," calls Jay when we return to the boiler.

"Good, thank you, boys."

"You're welcome," I say. "Isn't there anything else we can do?"

"No, not right now. Come back later and I'll let you shovel coal," Mr. Hackett says with a big grin. The sweat on his arms and face gleam in the light coming from the firebox door. Mr. Howard laughs at the joke. Jay and I know from last year it is not easy to keep the boiler fire-box fed when the boat is at full speed. The two men look funny together. One short and thin and one big and tall. They are like Doc and Uncle Ed in this regard.

We are soon warmed by our being near the hot boiler and return to the deck. The boat is almost to the tip of Bluff Point. We can see the end of the pier at Sturdevant's Landing as we come around the tip of land. There is a group of people waiting for the *Cricket* to arrive. They also want their first steamboat ride of the year.

"Lets look through Uncle's spyglass to see who is there," I say eagerly.

"Good idea," Jay exclaims.

"Uncle, may we use your spyglass?" I ask after we come into the small pilothouse.

"Of course, boys. Stand away from the wheel as I will be swinging her in soon."

"Yes, sir." Jay lifts the glass from its holder.

"Can you tell who is there?" I ask quickly. "Let me look."

Jay says, "Holy cow, the whole family is there. Here look."

I hold the glass to my right eye. Sure enough, Aunt Mertie and Jay's brothers and sister, my Ma, Ruthie, Mary and Carolyn and Mr. and

Mrs. Sturdevant are gaily waving to us from the pier. Jay carefully replaces the spyglass in its holder and we run to the lower deck. He and I stand by to help Mr. Stone with the gangway and greet our families as they step aboard.

"Hello," calls Aunt Mertie. "I see the launching of the *Cricket* was a success. You two boys look like you have been having a grand time on the boat."

"Yes, we have been," Jay answers. He has a big grin on his face.

"Did the launch go well?" Ma asks of Mr. Alvin Stone.

"Yes, Mrs. Lee. The boys were a good help and the launching went smoothly."

"You should sit inside, Ma. It's very cold on the open deck," I say as I help her off the gangplank.

"Yes, thank you Danny, that is a good idea. Come along girls," Ma says. Aunt Mertie escorts her two little boys into the cabin. Ma has her three girls in tow.

Mary hangs back and says, "I want to see the engines, Danny. And tell me what you did during the launch."

"All right. Step this way." I lead her into the engine room where we stand and watch the two churning steam engines.

"My, aren't they magnificent," Mary exclaims over the din of the machinery. "Do they work like the steam engine the thrashers bring with them, Mr. Hackett?"

"Yes, they do, Mary. They are more powerful as they have more work to do than just run a thrasher. It takes much power to push a big boat through the water."

"Oh, why is that?"

"This boat weighs a lot and the water resists being pushed aside by the boat. Each of these engines has a horsepower rating of twenty-five while a steam engine for thrashing might have only ten horsepower."

"My that is interesting, isn't it, Danny? How fast can the boat go?"

"Yes, it is." I am looking at my sister with admiration. She is interested in many different things as I am. "Didn't you tell me last year the boat's top speed is fourteen miles an hour, Mr. Hackett?" I ask.

"Yes, that's right."

"What does this thing do, Mr. Hackett?"

"You go ahead and tell her, Danny. I had better feed my boiler. I don't want to disappoint your uncle when he calls for more speed. Isn't that right, Howard?"

"That's for darn sure," exclaims Mr. Stone who has just come into the engine room. "Philo will want full steam for crossing the wide waters of the lake at the tip of the bluff."

The men begin to vigorously shovel coal into the firebox under the boiler. I pull Mary to one side and explain about the pressure gauge she had pointed at. "That gauge tells the engineer how much steam pressure there is inside the boiler. You see how this tube runs into the boiler?"

"What do the numbers mean?"

"Well, the pressure is measured in pounds per square inch." I hold my fingers for her to see what a square inch would look like. "You see this psi written on the face of the gauge? That is what it means. The steam pressure inside this boiler is 160 psi which is normal for full speed."

"Oh, yes, I understand," Mary says. A bright smile brought on by learning something new is on her face. Then a frown appears. "But why, what use is it to know the steam pressure inside the boiler?"

"A very good question, Sis. If the pressure becomes too low, the steam engines will slow and the boat will lose speed. If the pressure is too high, the boiler might blow up."

"Blow up," exclaims a surprised Mary. "Really?"

"Uncle Philo said it used to happen quite often but people are more careful now. If boats are being raced, the captains could become careless and disregard the danger."

"Mr. Stone, Mr. Hackett, have you ever seen a steam engine blow up?" Mary asks.

The men say, "No I haven't," between throwing shovel fulls of coal into the red-hot fire box. Mr. Stone adds, "Don't want to either. You'd best tell her about the safety valve, Danny."

"Huh, oh yes. This is a safety valve. It will open and let some of the steam pressure go if it is too high. Don't touch anything, Mary, as things here are very hot."

"So it isn't as dangerous as you made it sound is it, Danny?" Mary asks brightly.

"No, not unless the safety valves are wired shut."

"Wired shut!"

"Yes, some men would do anything to win a race."

"Oh, yes, I suppose some would. Tell me what you did at the launching, Danny."

"I helped set up the block and tackle with Jay and drove Bess and Kit."

"What did the horses do?"

"They pulled the boat into the water using the block and tackle for extra power."

"Really?" Mary exclaims again. "I don't understand how that is done."

I open my mouth to try to explain when a demanding, "Maaarrry, are you in there?" comes to us from the door that leads to the main deck of the *Cricket.*

"I'm coming," Mary replies. Out on the deck we face a very angry sister Ruthie.

"What were you doing in that dirty place?" she demands. "That is no place for a young lady."

"I, I, I was learning about the steam engines and the boiler," Mary stammers. "And talking to Mr. Hackett and Mr. Howard."

"Learning about that dirty, noisy, machinery? What for? Young ladies don't need to know about such things. In fact you shouldn't care about machinery."

"But but, I want to know about all kinds of things," Mary replies in a strong voice.

"You are being mean to our sister, Ruthie," I say. "I don't see why she shouldn't know about steam engines. They are very important to us and a wonderful source of power."

"I'm sure they are. It just is not right for a girl to be in such places. She shouldn't be interested in machinery. Things like that are for boys and men, not girls. Besides, Ma is wondering where you are. She sent me to look for you, both of you."

When we return to our families, Ma asks of Mary, "Where have you been?"

Mary answers, "We were in the engine room talking to Mr. Hackett and Mr. Howard."

"Look, Ma, Mary has gotten her nice coat dirty," Ruthie states. "You should be ashamed, Mary."

I look where Ruthie is pointing. There is a tiny smudge on Mary's red coat.

"I was just trying to learn about steam engines," Mary wails. "I'm sorry I got my coat dirty, Ma. I'll clean it when we get home."

"It is all right, Mary. It is a very little spot and will come out easily. I'll take care of it."

"She had no business going into the engine room and Danny should have known better than take her there," states Ruthie sharply. "What if someone saw her talking to Hackett."

"I asked him to go there with me," replies Mary boldly. "I want to know how steam engines work. Why shouldn't I talk with Mr. Hackett?"

"Ruth, I see nothing wrong with Mary wanting to know about steam engines. I am glad she is interested in learning about new ideas and having experiences other than house work. Modern girls should be knowledgeable about many things."

"But Ma, it isn't right for a girl to be interested in such things. She doesn't care a bit about sewing and such."

"She will when the time is right for her. I remember a time when all you wanted to do was play with the baby pigs."

"Oh, Ma did you have to tell Mary and Danny that?" Ruthie groans. Mary and I enjoy our big sister's discomfort.

"Never mind, Ruthie, Mary and I like baby pigs too," I say quickly. We have a good laugh then.

"Miss Ruth" Ma says sharply, "What is wrong with Mary talking to Mr. Hackett?"

"Well, I don't know, now that you ask. I just didn't think it was good for her," Ruthie says slowly.

Ma says sharply, "When you have a reason why Mary should not talk to Mr. Hackett you let me know."

"Yes, ma'am, you are right. I shouldn't have said that. There is nothing wrong with Mary talking to Mr. Hackett."

"Thank you, Ruth," Ma says with a sigh. "You still have not learned your lesson about generalizing about people. Have you?"

"I'm trying, Ma."

CHAPTER 10

▼

BRANCHPORT, PENN YAN AND HOME

We continue our trip around the bluff and head for Branchport. The water around the Branchport pier and boat basin is still thick with ice. We glide by and wave to folks who are on the pier. Aunt Clelli is there with cousins Anna and Carrie. I'm sorry they aren't on the *Cricket* with us.

I can see the *Earl* and several other small steamboats on shore. Soon they will ply the beautiful blue waters of Keuka Lake too.

The women and small children sit inside the cabin of the boat while Jay and I stand at the bow. Some of the Penn Yan boys have returned to be with us. The boy who laughed at me for liking Dr. Ball is not with them.

"Have you seen, Jimmy?" I ask.

One of the boys says, "He is at the stern with Baldwin."

"Who cares what they are doing," says Jay. "They're stuck up."

We continue around the lake along the west shore of the west branch. When we reach Pulteney Landing, we pick up a few more passengers and cross the lake to Sturdevant's Landing once again. There

Ma and Aunt Mertie prepare to leave the boat with the children. Mary wants to ride to Penn Yan with us and then ride on the hay wagon back home.

"May I go with Jay and Danny and ride home on the hay wagon?" she asks Ma.

"No, Mary, you may not continue to Penn Yan. You have on your best dress and coat. I don't want you to get them soiled while riding on the wagon."

"It is Sunday and you should act like a little lady today," Ruthie adds. "If you know how."

"But," says Mary her eyes bright with hope.

"I have spoken, Mary."

"Yes, Ma," Mary says dejectedly.

"I'll tell you about our adventures when I get home," I say.

"Phooey, you boys have all the fun," Mary exclaims angerly.

"Yah, we know," Jay and I say together. We are grinning the best we can. This makes Mary even more angry.

Uncle Philo stops the *Cricket* at several landings on the east side of the east branch of the lake before returning to Penn Yan.

The Baker and Amidon Folks are waiting on the Crosby Landing dock but do not signal Uncle Philo to stop. They wave as we slide by. I can see cousins Albert and Bea. Al is pouting as is his usual way but Bea is happily waving to us.

After school is out for the summer, the second week of June, the families who are related to us that live at Crosby will come to visit us by steamboat. Then in August will be the Baker Family Picnic that is held at the Assembly Grounds at Keuka Park.

Fenton's Landing is a short way north of Crosby Landing. Mr. George Fenton has a saw mill, basket factory and a fine old home on the hill overlooking the lake. There is no one waiting for us on Mr. Fenton's pier.

Uncle Philo will make one more trip around the loop as he has named it before calling it a day. In the summer, evening cruses are made but not this time of the year. The loop is the steamboat trip between Penn Yan and Branchport with stops between.

As the *Cricket* returns to the entrance of the channel that leads to Penn Yan, Uncle Philo asks Mr. Hackett for less speed. Soon we are moving very slowly along the route to the place we launched the boat in the morning.

When we arrive, the real challenge of large boat handling begins for the boat must be turned around in the channel. This is a very tricky maneuver as the channel in this area is only slightly wider than the *Cricket* is long. Uncle Philo and Mr. Hackett very carefully turn the boat and then ease it next to the pilings. This will be its birth for the boating season. Pa, Uncle Ed and Mr. Alvin Stone help direct Uncle

Philo as he steers the boat so it does not strike a bank of the stream. The *Cricket* is eighty-five feet long at the water line.

"All right boys, says Uncle Philo. Thanks for your help today and I hope you enjoyed your ride."

"We did," we say.

"We will meet often this summer, I'm sure," he smiles down on us. His dark beard, eyebrows and hair make him look severe but we know he isn't.

"Call on us whenever you need extra help," Jay replies. I nod my agreement. It is not work at all to be a deck hand on the *Cricket* or *Earl*. I hope he calls on me often.

"Please get the teams ready to go, Danny and Jay," Pa directs.

"Yes, sir," we say and run to get the teams. We help load the equipment onto the hay wagon and settle ourselves for the long ride home. Jay and I are setting on the backboard with or legs hanging off as before. We travel out the boat yard lane and turn left onto Elm Street.

A little shiver goes down my back as we drive past the cemetery. I can't help but shudder a little.

Of course Jay noticed, "You aren't afraid of cemeteries, are you?" he asks with a little laugh.

"Huh, no of course not. Are you? I was thinking of Grandpa and Grandma Lee buried there. That's all. There isn't anything wrong with that is there?" I try to cover up my fears with boldness so Jay won't know the truth.

"No nothing is wrong. I was thinking of our dead folks and wondered if you were too. Their grave site is just up that little lane, you know."

"Yes, I know. I have been there several times." I watch the big feet of the four draft horses clumping along behind us. The long white fur of our Belgians flies up with each heavy clomp though it is coated with dried mud.

I wonder what Grandpa and Grandma Lee were like. I bet they were very nice. I sure wish I had known them but they died the year I was born 1884. We sit silently until, part way up the Ridge Road hill, we hear....

"Hello! hello! help! Can you help, please?" calls a young woman as she runs toward us across a small pasture. She has gathered up her long skirts and is running very hard. Her sunbonnet blows off her head and hangs around her neck by its ribbon.

"Whoa," Pa shouts. "Boys, watch those teams."

All of us but Doc jump from the bed of the still moving wagon. The teams come to a stop but are not standing still as they should. They are surprised by their sudden stop in a place in the road where they have never been asked to stop before. They are being upset by the shouts of the running woman too.

Pa is holding Big Dan's bridle and stroking his face. Uncle Henry holds Jim while Uncle Ed helps Doc from the wagon. They, Jay and I calm the other teams. Quickly Uncle Henry vaults over the split rail fence and runs toward the distressed woman.

"What is the matter?" he calls.

"My husband! My poor husband!" she screams as she points toward their small dairy barn.

"This is the Newport place," Doc says to us. Concern marks his face. "A young couple. They have been here only a short while. Bought it from Mr. Retan."

The woman screams a high piercing cry and begins to collapse. Uncle Henry reaches her just in time to keep her limp body from striking the ground.

"What's the matter ma'am? What's wrong?" he asks cautiously.

We can barely hear her say, "In the barn. My husband. My husband is terribly hurt." She then gasps, "Please help him. He is in a bad way."

By this time the horses have become their usual placid selves. "The boys and I will stay here, you fellows go and see what the matter is," Doc says in his commanding voice. "Give us a call if you need us."

Pa and Uncle Ed quickly go to join Uncle Henry and the young woman.

"I wonder what is wrong?" I say to no one in particular. "Why can't we go now?"

Quietly, Doc says, "We will find out soon enough. Lots of bad things can happen in a barn as you know. Perhaps it is so bad your Pas won't want you to see it."

"Let's tie the teams to the fence posts so we can leave them if need be. They will be glad to have grass to nibble."

Jay and I look at each other in surprise. I had not thought about the man's predicament to be really bad. Perhaps the man is dead, gored by a bull or stuck in the chest by a pitchfork. I sure don't want to see anything like that. By the time we have the horses safely tied, everyone has disappeared into the barn.

I stand there looking at the barn hoping the situation isn't too awful but fearing the worst. Doc is trying to look unconcerned but I know he is. He is slowly rubbing Kit's neck. Bess is nuzzling his coat.

"Come on, we need your help," comes from the direction of the barn. It is Uncle Ed. He is motioning us to hurry.

We quickly crawl through the fence between the top and second rail. Jay and I take off as fast as we can while Doc trots along at his best speed.

As we enter the dark barn from the bright sunlight, I can't immediately see what is wrong. Then I see a large Holstein cow is lying on her side. That in itself is not unusual.

In a moment, when my eyes become accustomed to the dim light, to my horror I realize a young man is pined to the barn floor by the body of the cow. The cow is lying on the man almost covering him. All three of us let out a gasp of surprise and concern. Mr. Newport really is in serious trouble.

The man is softly moaning and Pa, Uncle Henry and Uncle Ed are looking at him. They must be trying to determine how to best get the cow off him.

Mrs. Newport is quietly sobbing.

"Doc, what do you think we should do?" Pa asks anxiously. "Have you ever experienced a situation like this? She must weigh at least fifteen hundred pounds."

"Why, yes, I have," Doc says slowly. Concern is on his face and fear is in his voice. He steadies himself by leaning on a barn floor post.

"What happened? What was the outcome?" Uncle Henry asks quickly.

"The man died," Doc answers quietly. "The man died."

Mrs. Newport utters a cry of despair and slowly sinks in a heap to the dirt floor of the barn.

"We must get the cow off without doing any more damage to him. He may not be hurt too badly laying in soft manure like he is," Doc observes. He rubs his hand over his forehead. His face shows worry.

Pa and Uncle Ed carry Mrs. Newport to one side and place her on a pile of clean straw. I look closely at the face of the cow and recognize a building panic.

"Look out," I say. "The cow looks like she is about to panic."

Uncle Henry steps back and says, "Soooo bossie, soooo bossie."

Sure enough the cow begins to thrash about. They are not the movements she would make if she were trying to get up though. The men grab her legs so she can't kick Mr. Newport who moans again. They are having difficulty keeping from being kicked themselves.

"Boys, sit on her neck and head," Pa directs.

We quickly do as we are told. I am sitting close to her face and realize her eyes are rolling and there is froth coming from her mouth. Her tongue is hanging to one side.

"Look, Pa," I say using a whisper. I don't wish to upset the cow any more than it already is.

"She is having a fit, hold on till it stops," Pa says. "Then we can pull her off him."

We restrain her the best we can.

In a few minutes she stops moving and begins to make a gurgling sound. I guess it is her breathing. Frothy liquid is coming from her nose and mouth. I want to get away from her but don't dare get up until told to do so. I look at Jay. He looks as fearful as I feel. Suddenly she begins to relax under us.

Doc sees this and quietly says, "Now is our chance. You boys push on her back and we will pull her legs."

We quickly get ourselves ready and Doc softly says, "Heave." The cow is off Mr. Newport.

While Doc, Pa and Uncle Henry examine the poor farmer, Jay and I look at the stricken cow. It seems to be asleep. She lies as still as death itself. I look more closely.

"She is dead!" I say to Jay. "Golly, I sure hope Mr. Newport has fared better." A feeling of dread rushes through me.

"I'll see if I can wake the missus," Uncle Ed says softly.

"I'm awake," comes weakly from Mrs. Newport. "How is James?"

Doc is feeling his arms and legs and examines his chest. "He isn't bleeding, his limbs seem all right. If he is hurt, it is serious 'cause it would be inside him. Newport, wake up. Wake up Mr. Newport." Doc gently shakes his shoulder.

Mr. Newport opens his eyes and says, "How is the cow?"

"Oh James, you are more worried about that old cow than you are yourself," Mrs. Newport exclaims as tears run down her face.

"Well, we do need a cow," Mr. Newport says.

"I'm afraid the cow is a goner," Doc answers. "How are you? Can you move?"

"Yes, I think so. I hurt all over but nothing too bad. No part hurts any more than another," he says bravely.

Mrs. Newport runs to his side and cradles her husband's head in her arms. She is quietly sobbing.

"Now, now, Martha. All is well except for the loss of our only cow."

"James, I am so worried and all you are concerned about is that old cow."

Mr. Newport begins to sit up and smiles tentatively. "It's a good thing I landed on the manure pile. It saved me."

"Don't try to stand up yet," Doc says. "Lean against me." The man thankfully leans against Doc's legs.

"I'll get some coffee," Mrs. Newport says.

"Martha's answer to everything is coffee," laughs the young farmer. When she returns, her husband is happily standing.

We drink our steaming coffee and eat slices of delicious bread and butter. "You make good butter, Mrs. Newport," Uncle Henry remarks.

"And good bread," I say with a smile.

"Thank you," says the embarrassed young wife.

"Guess she was your only cow," Pa says. It is clear there are no others in the barn.

"Yes, she was old when I got her but she was all I could afford. I had just bought this farm."

"I've got an extra and she is about to freshen," Pa offers.

"I've no money, Mr...."

"Lee, Mr. Newport. You are looking at some of the Lee Family of Bluff Point. We are all Lees except for this fine looking gentleman who is Zalmon Goodsell." Pa has his arm on Doc's shoulder. "Well, he has been with the family so long he is a family member too."

Doc is blushing with this introduction and scratching his boot toe into a small clod of dry manure. "Just call me Doc," Doc mumbles. The ends of his moustache are curling up.

"This is my brother, Henry and his son Jay," Pa continues. "This is another brother, Edward." The men raise their hats as Pa introduces them. "I am Charles and this is my son Danny."

"We are mighty pleased to make your acquaintance aren't we Martha?"

"Yes indeed we are. May I ask a question?" says a suddenly shy Martha.

"Of course, ask away," Pa says. A look of wonder is on his face.

"What were you doing with all those draft horses?"

"Martha. For shame. That's none of our business," Mr. Newport exclaims.

Martha Newport looks upset by this reprimand. She quietly says, "But James, you didn't see them coming up the road with three teams of beautiful horses and a hay wagon loaded with men and ropes and machines."

"Three teams? Machines? Now you have my curiosity up too."

"We were coming back from helping our other brother, Philo, launch his steamboat at Penn Yan," Uncle Ed explains.

"Oh, that makes things clear," Mr. Newport says. "The machines must be block and tackle and such."

"Yes, that is right. Brother Philo is the part owner of two steam-boats, the *Cricket* and the *Earl*. He is usually the captain of the *Cricket*."

"We will look for them when we need some lake transportation," Mr. Newport says. "Now, about your extra cow. As I said I don't have any cash but do have a willing pair of hands and a strong back."

"You can work the cow off. I'm glad to be rid of her as I don't really have room for her now."

"I'm much obliged, Mr. Lee. I'll do any work you have for me."

"Good trade then. We are the last farm south on the east side of the Ridge Road. Stop by when you are able and we will put you to work." Mr. and Mrs. Newport give each other a hug and us a pleasant smile.

We say our good-byes and as we walk toward the road I whisper to Jay, "We don't have any extra cow as far as I know." Jay just smiles.

CHAPTER 11

▼

THE WELL

At last the weather is warm and pleasant. Every day after school I help remove the brush from the apple, cherry and peach orchards after the men have done the trimming.

Pa won't let me do any of the trimming partly because my lack of height would make it slow and difficult and partly because Ma doesn't want me to climb the necessary ladders. I'm hoping to learn how to trim the trees next year. I'm sure I will be much taller then. I want to learn how to do the trimming to be of more help than just picking up the discarded branches. Fruit trees, like the grapevines, are trimmed to cause more and larger fruit to develop.

Everything goes well at school until Friday. It is afternoon recess. My fourth grade class is reading *The Land of Story-Books*, a poem by Robert Louis Stevenson. Rachel, Stan, and I take turns reading aloud. Rachel is a better reader than I am but not by much. Stan and I read at the same level. He is very upset by having to read aloud though. He sometimes makes mistakes because of this concern.

It is my turn to read to the whole school. Standing in front of all twenty-two students is embarrassing. I try to look and be casual about the situation. Reading to the class is not difficult I think to myself. I can do this well.

"*The Land of Story-Books*, by Robert Louis Stevenson," I read confidently.

> At evening when the lamp is lit,
> Around the fire my parents sit;
> They sit at home and talk and sing,
> and do not play at anything.
>
> Now, with my little gun, I crawl
> All in the dark along the wall,
> And follow round the forest track
> Away behind the sofa back.
>
> There, in the night, where none can spy,
> All in my hunter's camp I lie,
> And play at books that I have read
> Till it is time to go to bed.
>
> These are the hills, these are the woods,
> These are my starry solitudes;

I'm reading along smoothly until I come to the word solitudes which I miss pronounce as salitudes. All the older children laugh right out loud. Even Rachel laughs. My best friend, Stan doesn't laugh. He just looks at me with sympathy. I look up at teacher, and she too is amused by my mistake.

Ruthie at first laughs and then glowers at me from her side of the room. The side where the older children sit.

Miss Spaulding quickly becomes serious and corrects my mispronunciation. "Danny, the word is solitudes."

"Yes, ma'am, thank you," I say quietly. Then I continue reading by starting the sentence again....

> These are the hills, these are the woods,
> These are my starry salitudes;

But when I reach the offending word I am so nervous I mispronounce it again. Then, horrors of all horrors I choke on my spit and have to cough. By this time everyone in the classroom is laughing loudly. Boy, am I embarrassed. Mary comes to my aid by thumping me on the back.

"You may sit down, Danny," Miss Spaulding says in a kindly way. "Mary, please return to your seat."

"Yes, ma'am," Mary says.

I lay my head on my arms on my desk and try to clear my throat.

Mary and Stan give me a sympathetic look as teacher raps her ruler on her disk, "All right, children, the fun is over. Please continue reading, Stanley."

Poor Stan, he hates to be called Stanley and he hates to read aloud in front of the class. He slowly walks to the front of the room and manages to read the rest of the short poem without difficulty.

> And there the river by whose brink
> The roaring lions come to drink.
>
> I see the others far away
> As if in firelit camp they lay,
> And I, like to an Indian scout,
> Around their party prowled about.
>
> So, when my nurse comes in for me,
> Home I return across the sea,

And go to bed with backward looks
At my dear land of Story-books.

I am embarrassed by my mistake but mortified by the coughing spell that followed. At least it is Friday and perhaps everyone at school will have forgotten by Monday. Of course big sister Ruthie will not have forgotten. She is sure to make fun of me.

On the way home from school, Ruthie tells me how stupid I am and how embarrassed I made her feel. "You should be ashamed of yourself making such a dumb mistake," she says.

I don't think she was as embarrassed as I was. Once we arrive at home she right away tells Ma.

"He has done it again at school. He has made a fool of himself and embarrassed me in front of the whole class."

"What could he have done that is so terrible?" Ma asks.

Ruthie gleefully tells the sad tale. She likes it when I make a mistake at school so she can poke fun of me.

Ma gives me a kindly look and doesn't laugh at all. "Ruth, why must you be such a tattletale?"

"Why does he have to be such a goose?" Ruthie replies sharply.

"Hold your tongue, you are being disrespectful, young lady."

"I'm sorry, Ma. It is just that he is so immature."

"Your finding fault with him so much of the time is immature on your part. You must learn to be more tolerant. I don't like your attitude toward your only brother at all. He needs your support at school, not your ridicule. You must not make fun of him when he makes a simple mistake. You are much too critical of him. He is three years younger than you and should be able to look to you for support."

Ruthie says quietly, "Yes, Ma. I'll try." She is looking at the kitchen floor, shame is on her face. I note her face is getting red. It is her turn to be embarrassed.

I stand behind Ma and where only Ruthie can see me. Now is my chance to get back at my older sister. I make a funny face by sticking my fingers in my ears and looking cross-eyed. This makes her laugh and she gives me a little pat on the head.

"Nice try," she says to me as she leaves the kitchen with her long full skirt swishing behind her.

I hurry to do my chores and right after supper Mary, Carolyn, and I play catch in the backyard. We are using the red ball Carolyn received for Christmas. Carolyn can't throw or catch so we let her roll the ball to one of us and we roll it to her. She is pleased to have us playing with her. The ball doesn't roll very well in the thick heavy grass in our yard.

"When will I be able to catch and throw the ball like you do, Mary?" asks Carolyn after a particularly poor roll of the ball. "This is a bad way to have to play ball."

"You will need to practice a lot," Mary explains.

"But when will I practice if you always roll the ball to me?"

Mary looks at me with a what do I say now? look.

"When you are a little older, we will help you to learn to catch and throw the ball," I say.

"But I want to learn now," Carolyn whines.

"You will have to wait until you are larger and stronger just as we had to," Mary replies patently.

Carolyn stomps her foot, "But I don't want to wait. I want to play ball like you do now."

"All right, try throwing to me," I say.

Carolyn gets herself ready and with great determination tries to throw the ball to me. It only flies about four yards and hits the ground. I try not to laugh. One look at Carolyn tells me she is very angry and frustrated.

"That was pretty good," Mary says.

"Oh, was not," says disappointed Carolyn. "You said that just to make me feel better. I'll never learn how to throw a ball." She runs toward the house.

"You need lots more practice," Mary shouts after her.

"Sure you will. Mary and I had to learn how," I holler. I don't think she wants to practice.

Mary and I continue playing catch until almost dark. I understand how Carolyn feels about being too weak and small to do throw the ball well. She has my sympathy.

Golly, am I glad when it is time to go to bed because I want morning to come fast.

Saturday morning dawns clear with the promise of a nice spring day. There is just a little speck of light in the eastern sky when I arrive in the kitchen. I give Ma a good morning hug and she kisses me on the forehead.

"Good morning, Danny. It looks like it is going to be a fine day for your ride on Sally."

"Yes, I'm really excited. Most of the mud has dried and I just know I will find Captain Williamson's campsite today."

"I want to speak with you before you leave on your exploration."

"Yes, ma'am," I call as I quickly jump into my boots and coveralls.

I hear Mary come into the kitchen behind me. She puts on her work clothes and we walk as far as the poultry shed together. She is doing a good job with the poultry and doesn't need my help anymore. When she finishes with the chickens and turkeys, she works with me while I take care of the goats. She mostly plays with little Olive who is not so little anymore.

First thing yesterday morning, Mr. Copson of Branchport brought one of his billy goats for a visit with my does. In about five months Eleanor, Nellie, Gertrude, Lillian, and even Olive will produce baby goats. Boy, they will be lots of fun to play with.

Our Billy went to Branchport with Mr. Copson to be with some of his female goats. He has a humdinger of a little cart to carry goats from farm to farm. It is built very strong and even has a top to keep the goats from jumping out. There is room for four goats inside. The horse Mr. Copson is riding pulls the cart.

Mr. Copson has a small leather covered notebook he uses to keep a record of each goat transaction. It is important for his business that he knows which doe was with which billy and when.

Pa has already made a business deal with the goat man from Branchport for the sale of my young goats. It sure will be hard to give them up when the time comes. I dread it already. Perhaps Pa will let me keep one or two of them. I would have a larger heard then and more work to properly care for them. The extra effort would be worth it though as the goats are for me to make money with so I can take college courses after I finish high school. Ma is going to teach Mary and me how to make goat cheese so I can sell it too.

We have strict instructions to stay away from the visiting male goat. The billy goat seems nice enough now that he has finished checking out his temporary new housing in Billy's pen. He could change his attitude toward us very suddenly though. He could chase us and try to butt us with his horns. Not a pleasant thought. We don't want him to get away from us either. He could become lost.

Mary asks, "What is our visiting goat's name?"

"Don't know, didn't ask."

"Well, lets give him one," she says gaily. "He must have a name."

"You can if you want to but he won't be here very long."

"Oh, right, I forgot. No sense in giving him a name. Poohie."

"You can name all the baby goats," I say quickly. I was already thinking up names for the new goats but I will be a big brother and let Mary do it. It will be fun for her. She gives me a bright smile.

"Thanks, Danny. You can name the boy kids and I will name the girls."

"Good idea, Sis." Mary helps me by feeding the goats their mash and talks to me while I milk. The goats eat the same mash the cows do; ground corn, barley, and buckwheat. This we grind in our own windmill powered mill.

"It isn't fair that you have to sell the baby goats," Mary complains.

"What would we do with them if we didn't sell them?" I ask.

"I don't know. Just keep them to play with."

"Don't be silly, Mary. You know we must sell livestock to have money."

"Yes, I know. But it is sad to have to give up our friends."

"That is how things are done on a farm," I say as I give some hay to the visiting Mr. Goat. He looks quite mean now and I watch him carefully. He looks at me sharply with his large yellow eyes with the brown slit pupil.

I wonder how our Billy is doing at Mr. Copson's place. Wonder if he misses me. I hope he isn't afraid.

Mary goes into the house to help with breakfast while I finish my work.

Tabby, my favorite barn cat follows me around hoping I will have a hand out for him. I squirt some milk into a shallow tin bowl which he laps up greedily. The two other barn cats appear from nowhere and demand goat milk too. Soon they are all drinking milk from the same dish.

At the house, Ruthie takes the pail of steaming goat milk from me and I return to the horse barn to finish my other chores.

I eat my breakfast as fast as I can to have as much time as possible for exploring with Sally and looking for Captain Williamson's campsite.

"Now I don't need to tell you to be careful and pay attention to what you are doing do I Danny?" Pa asks sternly. "Watch where Sally is stepping so she doesn't stumble."

"No, sir, ummm, yes sir," I say quickly using as much emphasis as I can.

This conversation is a common event each time I am allowed to go off on my own. Guess Pa doesn't fully trust me not to make some kind of mistake. Come to think of it, I don't trust myself. I'm determined to have a good time with Sally while checking out likely cabin sites on the west side of Bluff Point. I know I will make no mistakes this time. What kind of problem could there be? I'll just be walking around in the woods.

"Here is your lunch," Ma says as she hands me a cloth wrapped package that is tied with a string. "I want you back by mid afternoon because we are expecting a visit from the Carter sisters who are retired teachers from Penn Yan. I want you to be here so the whole family will have a nice visit in the parlor. Your sister may stay with them when she moves to town to go to high school. We must give them a good impression of our family."

"I thought Ruthie was staying at the boarding house with cousin Ada," I say.

"Yes, that is possible. We hope staying with the Carter sisters will be less expensive than at the boarding house."

"Oh, I understand," I say thoughtfully. "You may have the money I make from selling my goat cheese and young goats. I don't know how much that will be but you and Pa are welcome to it."

"Thank you, Danny. That is very thoughtful of you. You are to save that money toward your own education after high school."

"Yes, I remember." Golly, education after high school. I have set myself the goal of taking a few college courses if possible. Perhaps I will study American history. I wonder what it will be like to go to college. It's a long time away. Just graduating from high school will be great. Most boys don't get a chance to go to high school as they are expected work in the family business. This is especially true of farm families and I am the only boy in my family.

Ruthie steps into the kitchen and with my eyes I tell her I don't want to visit with the Carter sisters. She pays me no attention and asks Ma which of her two good dresses she should wear during the visit. By the way she is prancing about you would think we were having a visit from President Cleveland and his wife.

I gather my lunch, jump into my boots and grab my jacket and hat from their hook in the kitchen.

In the horse barn I say hello to Bess and Sally. Of course I have already spoken to them when I did chores. Again I am disappointed that my little mare doesn't make any signs of friendship. She acts indifferent to me. I give her a carrot to munch, a few kind words and a little extra oats. She doesn't even wiggle an ear. Will she ever respond to me?

I wish there was something I could do to make her love me as I know good old Bess does. Bess always has a friendly nicker for me.

I saddle Sally, mount with the help of a potato crate and I am on my way. What a beautiful day to go exploring. Buster has gone to the wood lot with the men so I will not have his companionship. I will have Sally to talk to though. The weather is partly cloudy but not threatening.

I direct my horse south on the Ridge Road and turn west when we reach the beginning of Grandpa Scott's farm. There are many scrubby bushes and small trees so I let Sally pick her way. Jay was right when he said in January there was a lane here at one time. Without any snow cover it shows up quite plainly. I don't know why I hadn't seen it before. Wasn't looking for it, I guess.

We move along slowly and I keep careful watch of how the brush and trees look. Occasionally Sally and I get off the track but I can find it again. Our travel is slow and the mare seems to want to be doing something more exciting.

Several times I dismount to closely examine the ground for signs of a stone fireplace or the foundation of an old log cabin. I kick the dead leaves about to uncover any human works that might be there.

I must use a tree stump or large fallen log to help me mount Sally again. Still too short I moan to myself. But I am getting along all right.

I'm off my horse, looking at a likely spot. I can see a line of stones partly buried in the dry leaves and dirt. They are a pile of stones that look too organized to be natural and over a ways is another smaller pile. Hummmm. This spot looks very interesting. A big old red oak tree overlooks the beautiful place. I stumble over some half buried rotten logs. They look like their bark had been removed. The lake can be seen from here too. This would be a wonderful spot for a cabin.

The trees here about look like the lower branches have been cut off and to the left are some huge old pine trees. There are no other pine trees nearby so they may have been planted here.

I walk along slowly and look ahead to see the lay of the land. I am leading Sally by her reins. My mind is looking for cabin site clues. I find more half buried logs and another line of stones and larger rocks.

Suddenly there is a sharp breaking noise! I recognize it instantly as breaking wood. The ground at my feet is breaking under my weight! I am standing on an old leaf covered wooden top to something. It gives way and down I go into a deep dark hole in the ground. I have fallen into Captain Williamson's dug well! The old rotten planks of the well cover have given way.

I have found his campsite for sure! This is not how I wanted to find it though. Falling into a well is not a good idea under any circumstances. Here I am alone and in a deep cold hole in the ground. I was not paying attention to where I was stepping and have gotten myself into big trouble!

Fear of being in a dark place is coming over me. I must keep my head and not let my fear take control of my mind. My life depends on being able to think rationally. What should I do?

I'm not hurt, just a banged elbow, but I am standing in about two feet of very cold water. It is over the top of my boots. A shiver runs down my back as the cold wetness sets in. How do I get out of here?

Then I think of how long it has been since this well was used and the thought warms me. Captain Williamson's well is about one hundred years old! How exciting! He himself drew water from this spot. No wonder the boards gave way when I walked on them. I'll bet they were hand hewn. Perhaps by the famous man himself. How thrilling! A picture of Captain Williamson using the well comes into my mind. I feel better now.

Wait a minute I tell myself. You had better think about getting out of this hole. You can think about its history when you are on top of the ground once more. But how?

The walls of the well are made of rocks, layers of shale, clay, and dirt. I reach over my head and grasp a protruding rock with my fingers and try to pull myself up. This hurts my scrapped and bruised elbow but it must be done. I grit my teeth and pull hard with my hands as I try to find a place for my feet on the wall of the well. The rock I am hanging on to comes loose and all I accomplish is falling back into the water and getting more wet. I am showered with stones and dirt. Panic flows through my body in a flash. I might die here in this old well.

Get control of yourself! You can get out of here. Use your head.

I try again and again, each in a different spot. It's no good. The walls of the well are too soft and crumbly. My feet fail to find a grip in the slippery wet clay. I feel about over my head but find nothing for a solid handhold.

Jeepers, how am I going to get out of here? The well is only about eight feet deep but it might as well be a mile.

I can hear Sally stomping about. Then she whinnies. She must wonder where I have gone. Thump, thump, thump. I want to call her and tell her to go home but I can't take the chance she might step too close to the opening of the old well. She would knock dirt and rocks in on top of me. Or worse yet she might fall in too! Both of us would die here. Another cold shudder goes down my back. I am trapped!

What am I going to do? How am I going to get out of here? I want to scream and call for help but who would hear me? I try to pull myself up again and only succeed in cutting the palm of my hand on a sharp rock. Owowow! It is shale that breaks easily and leaves knife sharp edges. It will not hold my weight and just crumbles. I know my Pa and the other men will eventually come looking and find me but it could be too late.

I lean back against the dirt wall of the well and begin to shiver from the cold. I don't want to die.

Panic grows within me. I'm doomed!

Now I realize I can no longer hear Sally stomping and snorting above me. She is gone. I hope she has gone home but I doubt it. Home to her still is the Argyle place. The family has moved. The house and barns are empty. There is no one there to tell my Pa about the free running horse. There is no one there to tell my folks something is wrong.

I'm alone and unable to save myself. Oh, why didn't I look where I was walking?

I look at my dirt caked bleeding hands in the half-light. They are very sore. I feel so helpless and hopeless. I'm cold all over now. Not just my feet and legs. Cold shivers spread over my body. My teeth are chattering. Looking up through the hole in the old planks all I can see are a few leafless tree limbs and the sky. The location of the sun tells me it is afternoon.

I know crying won't help but I feel the tightness in my throat and prickling in my nose that tells me I am about to cry. I let the tears come. Oh, what am I to do? Pa and the men will look for me but by the time I'm found I could be dead from the cold and wet.

CHAPTER 12

▼

LITTLE BIRD

Sometime goes by, I don't know how much. Then, something makes me look up. I don't remember hearing a noise though.

Yikes! There is a face looking down at me. A round brown face.

"Hello, do you want to get out?" the face asks.

"Yes, I do. Please get me out of here," I call. I hope this person didn't hear me crying.

Without another word the face is gone. Who is this person I wonder? Where did he come from? What is he doing on this part of Bluff Point? I guess I don't care as long as he gets me out of this hole in the ground.

Time goes by slowly. It seems as if I have been waiting forever. Then I hear the soft crunch, crunch of foot steps in the dead leaves. I am struck on the head by something. I grab hold and see, in the half light of the well, it is a length of thick wild grapevine.

"Hold on," comes from above.

I hear some thrashing about and feel the length of vine tighten. I make my grip as hard as I can and quickly find myself on my belly at the edge of the well. A hand pulls me to my feet and I see my rescuer in his entirety.

He is an Indian boy who is about my age. He is dressed in long pants that have fringe down the outside of the legs. His over shirt is long and has fringe too. The boy's shirt and pants are a tan color with dark green fringe. He has on a small green hat with a turkey feather coming from it. He also has a leather belt that holds a beaded knife sheath. Inside the sheath is a large knife.

There is a look of concern and wonderment on the Indian boy's face.

"Hello, my name is Danny Lee. Golly, am I glad to see you. I thought I was a goner."

"I am called Little Bird. Are you all right?"

"Pleased to meet you, Little Bird. Yes, I'm fine now."

"What were you doing in that hole? Didn't you know it was there?" Little Bird asks sharply. As if I had done something very stupid on purpose. "It is an old well."

"Ah, no, I didn't know it was there."

"I have been by here many times and knew of the well."

"Oh, ummm, yes. Thank you for saving me," I say with a smile. "You are welcome. Where do you live? Does this horse belong to you?"

There, tied to a nearby tree quietly stands Sally. She is looking at me and nickers softly. "Yes, that is my horse. How did you find her?"

"She came walking up to me and I followed her to you. I wanted to find who she belonged to."

"Good, Sally! Good girl! You did help me after all. She is new to our family and I didn't know what she would do if loose."

I walk up to her and give her a hug and pat on her neck. For once she doesn't pull away from me. She nickers again. Her ears are pointed toward me. My mare acts as if she is glad to see me.

"Oh gosh, look what time it is," I say as I find the sun through the leafless trees. "It is mid afternoon. I was supposed to be home before this. Would you like a ride on Sally? I must stop at my house and then I could take you home. I don't live far."

"Ummm, I guess that would be all right. I would like to see what your house is like."

"I'm sure my Ma will have milk and cake for us. I haven't had lunch. Would you like half my beef sandwich?" I pull my cloth wrapped sandwich out of my coat pocket. It is a little squashed from my recent activities of trying to get out of the well.

"Mummm. Sounds good," my rescuer says with a slight smile and bright black eyes.

Little Bird is taller than I am and has no trouble pulling himself onto Sally's back. I lead her to a pile of rocks. They look as if they could have been a stone fireplace a long time ago. I feel foolish having to stand on something to mount my horse.

"You can't get on this little horse without standing on pile of rocks?" Little Bird asks. He sounds like my sister Ruthie.

"No, not yet, but I will be able to soon. I just need to be a little taller."

"You need to be a lot taller if you are going to climb up like your horse is a tree."

"What do you mean?" My feelings are hurt but I will not let Little Bird see. I'm sure he means well.

"Let me show you an easier way to get on your horse," he says as he slides down her side.

Little Bird leads Sally away from the pile of rocks. "Hold the reins in your left hand. Then jump up, grab the saddle horn with both hands and at the same time stick your left foot into the stirrup." He demonstrates, "See, it is easy." Then he slides off again.

"I'll give it a try," I say with determination. I sure hope I can do this. After making a mighty leap up, I find myself standing on the stirrup with Sally starting to walk away. I throw my leg over her back and take my seat. "Whoa, Sally." Wow! I'm a success.

"Hey, Little Bird, that is a jim-dandy way to mount a horse. How did you learn?"

"My father."

"Does your family live around here?"

"Yes, we live near the place you call Branchport," Little Bird explains.

"You do? I didn't know there were any Indian families around here."

"We haven't been here long. We call ourselves the Seneca People."

"Seneca People, all right. What does your father do for a living?" I ask. "Is he a farmer?"

"He is dead. The smallpox got him."

"Oh, I'm very sorry," I say slowly.

"Thank you, he has been gone for quite awhile now. I live with my grandfather and my mother."

"We can talk as we ride, come on up," I say as I remove my foot from the left stirrup and extend my hand to Little Bird. No sooner than I have done this than my new friend is sitting behind me. "Get going, Sally, I have to get home quickly." I share my lunch with Little Bird.

Sally carefully picks her way through the young trees and brush. Little Bird and I must be ready to duck under overhanging tree limbs.

Little Bird explains that he and his mother are living with his grandfather who wishes to spend his last days near Branchport. He calls the place Da Goh nuhn Da Gay which means two lakes.

"Why is that?" I ask.

"It is because his ancestors lived around here many years ago."

"Oh, I understand."

Sally carries us cautiously through trees and brush until we reach the Ridge Road. Then I touch my heels to her sides and say, "Giddap girl," and we are off like the wind. When we reach our yard, I know I am in for trouble as there is a buggy inside the horse barn. An old looking black horse is tethered near the well used buggy. She is unharnessed. Putting up the horse and buggy would have been my job and I wasn't home to do it.

Regret flows through my body. I have failed to do as I was told again. I should have been more careful and not fallen into the old well. If I had used my head, I would have known there had to be a well in the area. Looking for the danger of an old dug well should have been foremost in my mind.

We slide off Sally and I give her some hay and water. I motion Little Bird to follow me and remove my wet and muddy boots in the wood-shed. Stockings I hang on a nail to dry. My new friend does not need to remove his moccasins. How he has kept them so clean I don't know. I step into the kitchen with Little Bird right behind me.

Ma is standing just inside the door, hands on hips. She must have seen us arrive.

"Why are you late, Danny? We were worried. Hello, who is this?"

I quickly pull Little Bird along side of me. "I'm sorry I'm late, Ma. This is Little Bird. He is a Seneca Indian. He pulled me out of Captain Williamson's well."

"This is going to be a silly question but, how did you get in Captain Williamson's well?"

"I fell," I say like it was an everyday occurrence.

"Oh, I assumed as much. Thank you for helping Danny, Little Bird."

"You are welcome, Danny's Mother."

"You aren't hurt are you?" Ma asks with worry in her voice.

"No, I'm all right. Just wet and a little banged up."

"Let me see," says my concerned Ma. "These cuts and scrapes on your hands need a good washing. I'll get some hot water."

"Thanks, Ma."

"The Carter sisters are here, Danny. Since they arrived late, they are going to spend the night with us. Please change your clothes and make yourself presentable. Wash your feet and legs too."

"Yes, ma'am. I promised Little Bird I would take him home, Ma. He and his family live over by Branchport."

Just now Ruthie comes into the kitchen. I am sitting on the kitchen stool washing my feet and legs.

She gives me a very stern look and says coldly, "It makes no difference to me that you weren't here to greet the Carter sisters. In fact I am glad. You won't have as much time to embarrass me this way." She pokes her nose into the air and says, "Why did you bring home this Indian boy? Don't bring him into the parlor."

"RUTH MILDRED LEE!" exclaims Ma. It is a hushed but stern voice. She doesn't want the ladies in the front parlor to hear. "For shame. You apologize to Little Bird immediately." I have seldom seen my Ma look so angry. "You are a thoughtless young lady."

"Ahmmmm. I am very sorry I said that, Little Bird. Please accept my sincere apology." Tears are forming in Ruthie's hazel eyes. She knows she has been very rude.

Little Bird looks at me with wonder on his face. I don't know him well but his feelings must be hurt.

"Please don't let my big sister's words hurt you. She likes being mean to me too," I say as I finish drying my feet and legs.

Ruthie's face is contorted with worry. "I was wrong when I spoke to you like that, aaah, Little Bird. I was very thoughtless and ill-mannered."

"It is all right, Danny's Sister. You are not the first white person who has not wanted me around," Little Bird says slowly and carefully. His face shows no expression.

"Oh, Ma, what am I to do? Will I never learn to think about other person's feelings before I speak?"

"We all must remember that words spoken can't be retrieved. We will begin again to meet Little Bird. Is that all right with you, young man?" Ma asks. "A friend of Danny's is always welcome in this house."

"Yes, ma'am."

Quickly I say, "Ma and Ruthie, this is my new friend, Little Bird. Little Bird, this is my mother, Mrs. Lee and this is my big sister, Ruthie."

"Welcome to our home, Little Bird," Ma says.

"Pleased to meet you, Little Bird," Ruthie says with her best smile. She offers her hand, which Little Bird takes and solemnly shakes. "Where did you meet my brother?"

"At the old cabin place near the shore of the lake." He looks at me with a small grin on his face but doesn't say a word about my falling into Captain Williamson's well.

"Oh, wonderful, you found the place then," Ruthie says to me. "Good for you." Ruthie has the most pleasant smile on her face I have ever seen. I wonder what has gotten into her. She must feel extremely bad about what she said to Little Bird.

"Danny, after you have finished washing, please change into clean school clothes," Ma says. "Then we will all go into the parlor and have cake and tea. Or would you rather have milk, Little Bird?"

"Milk would be nice, thank you," my new friend says politely.

I take Little Bird to my room and let him look at my treasures while I change my clothes. He says he likes my orange box with the black figures on it. I see him looking at the Indian designs. I wonder what he thinks of them.

"We will spend a short time in the house, Little Bird. The family has guests and it is polite for us to make an appearance."

"I understand," says Little Bird. "It would be the same if we were at my house."

"Good, I will ride you home on Sally as soon as I can." Then we join everyone in the guest parlor. When we step into the room, Pa introduces me to the Carter sisters and I introduce Little Bird to everyone.

Mary and Carolyn are sitting on little stools just inside the room. They look at Little Bird in amazement but say nothing. They know this is an adult gathering and children are to be quiet unless they have something to say that is of interest to all or are spoken to by an adult.

I sit on the floor next to the girls and whisper to my new friend to do the same.

The Carter sisters are sitting on the sofa. Pa is standing on the other side of the entrance to the parlor. He has on his Sunday suit and looks to me as though he wished he were any place else.

Mary and Carolyn look pretty in their Sunday dresses and are sitting quietly, hands on their lap. Soon Ruthie comes into the room and gives each of us a napkin and a small plate and fork beginning with our lady guests from town. I neatly place the white cloth on my lap. Little Bird watches and does the same.

Ruthie returns with a platter of little cakes which she offers to each person around the room. I carefully try to pick up my cake solely with my fork but find I must steady it with my finger. Ruthie then places the platter on the walnut tea table. I can see Little Bird eyeing the little cakes in anticipation. They are Ma's fancy sugar cakes. They aren't very large but are very delicious. My big sister hands each of us children a glass of milk. She gives me a look I know means, don't spill it. Ma sits at the small table and pours tea for the adults.

We sit quietly, munch cake, carefully sip milk and listen to the adults talk. Then I feel Little Bird touching my leg. I know he must go home. "Excuse me, everyone," I say when no one is speaking. "Little Bird and I must leave. He has to go home." I feel all eyes on me. My face flushes with embarrassment as I stand.

"Of course, your friend needs to be given a ride home. I will ride along with you," Pa says. "It will be dark soon."

I am sure Pa wants to get out of the house and away from the ladies' parlor talk. The Carter sisters nod their understanding.

CHAPTER 13

▼

THE STORY OF RED JACKET
(SA GO YE WAT HA)

We ride toward Branchport, Pa on Toby and Little Bird and me on Sally. What a pleasant way to end an afternoon. The sun is low in the western sky. We will have enough light to reach Branchport. Riding home in the dark will be an adventure.

Little Bird directs us to the old path down the side of the bluff, leaving the Ridge Road behind before we normally would turn west. Then, a few miles before we reach Sugar Creek which is the inlet to the lake, Little Bird points out a narrow path into the woods.

"This is the way to our house," he states.

We make the turn and soon find ourselves in a large clearing with a small one story house in the center. The main part of the house is square with a rectangular wing to the left side. The whole building is sided with unpainted boards. It has wooden shingles on the roof. Behind the house is a log building to shelter the livestock. Land on the right side of the house has already been prepared for a large garden.

A woman comes to the door to greet us. We quickly dismount and Little Bird introduces her to us as his mother, Quiet Bird. She is obviously happy to see her wandering son. She is wearing a long dress and over shirt that is made of the same material as Little Bird's clothes.

"You were away a long time, son. Your grandfather and I were beginning to be worried about you."

"I'm sorry Mother," Little Bird says. "Danny needed my help."

My Pa quickly says, "It is our fault he has returned home so late, Mrs. Bird, he helped my boy and came to our house for a short while."

"It is kind of you to bring him home," she says while giving Little Bird a big hug.

"It was the neighborly thing to do. We didn't know anyone was living here. The place had been empty for quite sometime."

"We have been here only a short while," Quiet Bird says.

We are invited into the house and asked to sit on a low couch. Sitting on another couch is a very old man who is introduced as Little Bird's grandfather, Flying Owl.

I have to admit I am very nervous about meeting this family. What am I to say to them? How should I act? They are so very different from my family. My Pa has no such problem and is soon chatting away with Quiet Bird and her father. He speaks as he would to any person he had just met.

"Your son helped my son out of a very difficult situation this forenoon, Quiet Bird. Danny had fallen into an old well in the woods near the tip of the bluff and Little Bird pulled him out. You sure have a resourceful boy here," Pa says with a smile. He gives Little Bird a pat on the back.

Flying Owl nods his agreement.

"Yes, Little Bird is like his father and knows how to deal successfully with a problem," says Quiet Bird who is busy at a cook stove in the center of the room. Soon she hands us steaming bowls of chicken stew. Little Bird and I grin at each other as we shovel in the delicious stew.

All we had since breakfast was half a beef sandwich, milk and cake. Good but not nearly enough for growing boys.

Quiet Bird helps her father with his bowl of food and after we finish eating she tells us a little about him.

"My father goes by the name of Flying Owl because he prefers to think events over before acting. He quietly makes his plans and then acts." Again the old man nods his agreement.

Quiet Bird explains that the Seneca People have a strong belief in dreams and her father had dreamed he was to die near where the famous Seneca orator, Red Jacket, was born and grew up. That place is a few miles south of Branchport on the west side of the lake. The Seneca name for Red Jacket is Sa go ye wat ha which means he keeps them awake.

"There is a marker, a big rock, that shows the place where Red Jacket's mother is buried. Have you seen it?" Flying Owl asks in a mixture of English and Seneca words. Quiet Bird explains the Seneca words to us.

My Pa says, "Yes, I have, Flying Owl." I look at my Pa in surprise. He has never told me of this. Pa says to me, "I will show you the place the next time we go to visit Philo. The spot is a mile or so south of his house."

Flying Owl slowly tells us of his dream.

"It was one night last year when I was suddenly aware of a figure standing over me as I slept. He was a very tall person in a white man's red jacket and deer skin leggings. A large silver metal hung on a silver chain around his neck. He spoke in a bold clear voice, *I want you to go to your final resting place where my mother and father lived and where I grew up. It is the place called Da Goh nuha Da Gay'.*"

"The amazing image remained there for a moment or two and then slowly drifted away. I was very frightened by the figure and startled by his words when I awoke."

"We were living on the Allegany Reservation at the time. I had planned on living out my days there. As my family is descended from

Sa go ye wat ha, I decided it would be good to go to Da Goh nuha Da Gay and live where I could be near his spirit. We are both of the wolf clan. I could not go against the wishes of Sa go ye wat ha."

"He was called Otetiana as a young man because of his great skill in carrying messages on foot across the territory. You see, we didn't have written messages like white people. The information must have been remembered and carried from place to place by runners." Flying Owl stops to rest.

"Grandfather, please tell us more about Red Jacket," Little Bird asks.

Flying Owl settles himself on his couch and begins telling more of the stories of Red Jacket.

"Red Jacket was born in the family cabin in the territory called Da Goh nuha Da Gay in 1752. The family lived there until he was twelve years old. The town was used mostly in the summer as the land was good for gardens and hunting. As he grew older Sa go ye wat ha became famous for being a very fast runner and was asked to carry messages from one Seneca town to another. His speed and skill at remembering the messages soon made him much in demand."

"He was about twenty-three years old when the Americans began to fight the English to establish their own government. The English had given the Iroquois People tools made from iron that were much stronger than our stone or wooden ones. They had given us cloth blankets that were much warmer than the animal skins we had been using. They had given us iron pots for our women to boil our food in. Pots that did not break like our old pots made of clay. The English had given us guns that made supplying our families with meat much easier. Over many years the Iroquois People became dependent on the English for everyday things."

"The English sent religious leaders to help us learn about Christianity. These good people also wrote down our words so we would have a written language like white men. The Iroquois People got along well with the English people."

"The American people treated us well too. They helped us with supplies when they found we were in need. They too helped us learn about Christianity. We were living together in friendship. The Americans sent blacksmiths to live among us to teach us how to mend and make iron tools."

"Both the English and the Americans traded with us for animal pelts and our families had many good things we would not have had without this trade."

"Then the war came. It changed everything. We Iroquois People had difficulty understand why the Americans were fighting the English King who had been very kind to us for so long. English army officers wanted us to fight the Americans. The Americans wanted the people of the Iroquois Nation to remain neutral in the war."

"This conflict brought many problems to our people. We were being pulled in two directions. The Americans began to supply us with more goods so we would not fight them. But we felt very loyal to the English who had been our friends for so long. What were we to do? Our people were caught in the middle of a great war. Our leaders were pulled first toward the English and then toward the Americans. The situation was awful for the Iroquois People for it split us into many groups. We were no longer the proud Six Nations of the Iroquois Confederacy."

"Many Mohawk, Seneca, Onondaga and Cayuga men fought for the English. Many Oneida and Tuscarora men fought for the Americans and other of our people remained neutral."

"Sa go ye wat ha carried messages for the English army. This was a very important trust. He was given a red army coat for this service. From that time on he was called Red Jacket. He did not fight in the war until Seneca Nation lands were invaded by the white armies and he was defending his home. Red Jacket became a Seneca Chief by his own efforts not as a warrior but by being a diplomat. He was a sachem or peace chief."

"Many very bad things were done by white people to Indian people and many very bad things were done by Indian people to white people during the war."

"When the war was over in 1783 and the Americans had won, the members of the Iroquois Nation were considered a defeated enemy by the Americans. They lumped all of the Indians together whether they fought on the side of England or not. It was at this time Sa go ye wat ha became a strong voice in the defense of his people against American demands for Indian land. Despite of the efforts of Sa go ye wat ha and others of our leaders, much of our land was taken from us."

"Sa go ye wat ha was one of our young leaders who spoke for us at the Fort Stanwix Treaty Council in the fall of 1784. At this council, peace was declared between our people and the American government. Even the American leaders were impressed by Sa go ye wat ha's oration and ability to present facts clearly and fairly."

"I will tell the story of Sa go ye wat ha at the Fort Stanwix 1784 Peace Treaty as it has been passed down through generations of Seneca wolf clan members."

"During an Iroquois Council fire it was decided Red Jacket and Cornplanter; who was a great war chief, would represent the Seneca Nation at the Fort Stanwix Treaty Council. They and their party of twenty warriors, women, and children moved from their homes near Fort Niagara in western New York State. They moved mostly on foot to Fort Stanwix located at the Oneida Carry, the portage between the Mohawk River and Wood Creek which leads to Oneida Lake."

"The family groups traveled quickly using canoes in streams and lakes wherever possible. They only stopped briefly to eat and sleep at night. Some families in the party were Seneca of the Wolf clan. Other families were members of the other Seneca clans, Bear, Beaver, Turtle, Snipe, Hawk, Heron, and Deer. They would be joined at Fort Stanwix by representatives from the Mohawk, Onondaga, and Cayuga nations who had also sided with the British during the recent war."

"Travel was easy for these people as there was a well-worn path to follow. They were used to traveling great distances on foot and in streams with canoes. The weather was cool and dry in mid September and a rapid pace was set. Where streams or lakes could be used, canoes were made available by local members of the Iroquois Confederacy. These people also contributed food and offered a place to sleep as the Seneca delegation passed through their lands."

"Some of the Seneca men went ahead of the main group to prepare housing for the women and children. Red Jacket and this group arrived at the fort after five days of travel. They found many Indians camped outside the newly reconstructed fort which now consisted of three log blockhouses joined by a log palisade. Members of the Oneida and Tuscarora Nations were there too. These tribes had fought alongside the Americans during the war."

"The men were greeted by barking dogs, children, and soon Indian men and women from the encampment. The Seneca delegation members were given a place to put their few belongings and everyone helped build huts to house their families. A feast and council fire were planned for the next night."

"Red Jacket felt it was his duty to draw the Indians together so they could speak as one nation, the powerful Iroquois Confederacy. Together they would have more ability to influence the outcome of the conference."

"In the meantime the newly arrived Senecas decided to look around the fort and, if they could, meet their white opponents and fellow Iroquois. First they adorned themselves with beads and special headdresses that denoted their status as chiefs of the Seneca People."

"The entrance to the palisade was open so Red Jacket, Cornplanter and several Seneca young men walked right in. Once inside, they were challenged by a young white man who was dressed in the blue and buff of a regular American soldier."

*   *   *   *

"What do you want in here?" he asks sharply.

Cornplanter answers carefully, "We are of the Seneca Nation. We have come to talk with your government men."

The young man gives them an understanding look and says, "Follow me." He walks into the nearest blockhouse and leads us up some steep stairs. Cornplanter is followed by Red Jacket and the young Seneca men. The youngest man is at the end of the line. His name is Tall Feather and he will tell us what he learns and sees.

There are three rooms on the second floor, two smaller ones and large one. We are led into the large room but we look with curiosity into the small rooms as we pass the open doorways.

"That must be where the white men sleep," Tall Feather says to his companions.

"Yes," says one of the men. "Look how strange their sleeping platforms are. They are thick with blankets and soft things. These men must be soft to need such sleeping platforms. They will be easy to talk to. We will win in the negotiations, I am confident of this."

Red Jacket speaks, "You must not think the negotiations will be easy, Running Bear. Just because they like to sleep in a soft bed, does not mean the American government men will treat with us fairly. We will have to be on our guard every moment."

I, Tall Feather, stand looking at the strange things the white men have. There are food containers on wooden shelves, and bundles pushed under the lower sleeping platform. There is a lump of something soft at one end of both sleeping platforms.

We move into the large room and stand to one side. This room also has a sleeping platform but it is much larger than those in the small rooms. It is even more strange to look at as it is high off the floor and very thick. It stands on four wooden legs that almost reach the ceiling of the room. Most puzzling of all is there is a cloth top and side curtains attached to the bed. What strangeness is this?

I begin to laugh but Running Bear pokes me in the chest with his finger and says, "Be quiet Tall Feather, you are only here to listen and learn, not to be heard."

I remember to keep my thoughts to myself after that. In the center of the room is a long table with chairs around it. There is a large brick fireplace on the wall opposite the door. Next to the fireplace is a small table with stacks of books and papers on it. An American chief must live in this room.

Soon we hear loud clumping steps coming up the stairs. In a moment three white men stroll into the room. These very hard looking men introduce themselves as Oliver Wolcott, Richard Butler, and Arthur Lee, Commissioners from the United States Congress.

Oliver Wolcott speaks, "We are ready to negotiate with the representatives of the Iroquois Nation. Let us meet at midday tomorrow. We do not want to talk to each Indian Nation individually." Oliver Wolcott was very cold and spoke harshly. "Representatives of the State of New York will also be talking with you to settle their differences. These will be tough and very serious negotiations as you Indian people have much to answer for."

Red Jacket says, "We are ready to listen to what you have to say. We hope you will listen to what we have to say. We wish to speak as the Iroquois Nation. We are not the only people who have much to answer for. Many American men conducted themselves fiercely against our women and children."

Oliver Wolcott mumbles a reply that is not at all friendly. "We shall see who will answer for the disgraceful hostilities between the Indians and the American families."

I look at Cornplanter's face. It is fierce and angry.

As the Seneca men leave the compound Cornplanter speaks to Red Jacket, "The white men are going to treat us as the enemy and punish us for siding with the English. They are going to blame all the Iroquois for violence against their families. They have taken control of all the land the English held."

"Yes," says Red Jacket. The other Seneca men gravely nod their heads. "It is true, we were at war with the Americans. Many of us were their enemy. What will become of those of the Iroquois Nation who were not at war with the Americans?" asks a wise Red Jacket. The others are without an answer. "Who will be punished for the murder of women and children of both sides?" Again there is no answer.

By the time the family huts were finished on the second day, the rest of the Seneca Nation representatives arrived at Fort Stanwix. Preparations are then made for a great council fire.

There are many speakers. Everyone listens to what others have to say. Some are war chiefs and others are sachem chiefs. When it is the turn for Red Jacket to speak, everyone is hushed and listens respectively as he is known as a skilled orator. He speaks for Iroquois unity against the Americans. "We must speak with power. We must not let the Americans take our land." Everyone sits around the council fire and eats boiled meat and squash.

The next day one small canon is fired to mark the beginning of the Peace Conference. Red Jacket's oratory at their council fire had made it clear to the Iroquois that the demands of the Americans would punish many innocent Indian groups and this was not acceptable. They also did not want to give up their lands to the Americans. This, however, was not to be.

The 1784 treaty at Fort Stanwix declared peace between the Americans and Indians and set the western boundary of the Six Nations. The Ohio Territories would no longer be under the control of the Senecas. As the Indians would lose much land, Red Jacket did not accept the treaty.

Cornplanter urged acceptance of the treaty as the best that was possible. Boundaries were drawn for the Iroquois.

In the treaty the Americans lumped all the Seneca, Mohawk, Oneida, Onondaga, Tuscarora and Cayuga people together though some remained neutral and others fought against the British. Indians lost much of their lands as the Americans claimed all the land once held by the British. Some Indians were paid for their land with cheap goods. But by this time the members of the Six Nations were so poor there was not much room for negotiation. They needed so many things for their families they traded away their land to get them.

*   *   *   *

Flying Owl has put down his empty bowl and sits with his head bowed. "All we have left of a once great nation is a few acres of land the American government calls reservations. We are prisoners on our own land. Soon I will be with my ancestors and will not have to see what has become of the Seneca People."

I take the hand of Little Bird in mine and give it a small squeeze. I hope he understands I truly feel sad that Flying Owl has come here to die. "But Flying Owl, the Seneca People will always be a great people no mater where they are living."

Flying Owl smiles a weak smile.

"Well, Son," Pa says. "We had best be going home. Your Ma will be wondering where we are. Thank you for your hospitality, Quiet Bird. Thank you Flying Owl for telling us about Red Jacket."

"Don't fall into any more wells, Danny," calls Little Bird.

"I won't," I say with a smile. Little Bird is smiling too. "See you around Branchport sometime."

"Yes, I'll be looking for you."

Pa and I walk to our horses. Sally gives me a quick look and a soft nicker as I come up to her. I'm very glad she recognizes me. Pa watches with surprise as I mount Sally the way Little Bird taught me. He looks pleased.

We are on our way. I look up at the sky; there are no stars to be seen. It must have become cloudy while we were with Little Bird's family. The moon has not risen so it is very dark. We will have to rely on our horses to keep to the track. Slowly my eyes adjust to the darkness and it becomes easy to follow Toby's light gray rump. When we reach the Ridge Road, I pull alongside Pa and we ride together. The darkness doesn't bother me. I guess it is because I'm so pleased with finding a new friend in Little Bird. I'm also pleased Sally is greeting me when she sees me.

Pa is quiet for a long time, then he softly speaks, "I sure enjoyed listening to Flying Owl talk about the old days. I hope you did too."

"Oh, yes. I learned a lot about the Seneca Indians and Red Jacket. It is exciting to know he lived near Branchport when he was my age."

"Many people don't give much regard to our native people but I want you to treat this family with the respect they deserve. You can have a wonderful friend in Little Bird."

"Yes Pa, I will. I like Little Bird a lot already."

"Good. Let's get going. We have chores to do when we arrive home."

We urge our horses into a trot. I can tell Sally is enjoying her freedom to run. When we reach the top of the hill, and are only about half a mile from home, Pa suddenly puts Toby into a full gallop. I touch my heels to Sally's smooth sides and she leaps forward. She is no match for the much taller Toby and Pa beats us to the horse barn by several lengths. I am happy with myself that I could keep my small body correctly balanced in my too large saddle.

As we fly past the house, I can see the little face of Carolyn peeking out at us. Our arrival will be announced for sure.

Ma meets us at the woodshed door, "What kept you two? We expected you home before dark."

Pa explains that we visited with Little Bird's family and learned about the Seneca Indians of long ago.

"We have eaten. I have kept dinner warm for you two. Please hurry along with your chores. I think our guests are tired and wish to go to bed."

Pa takes out his pocket watch, "But Ellen, it is only half past six."

"It has been a long exhausting day for them Charles."

"Oh, yes, I suppose it has." He looks puzzled.

We change into work clothes, pull on clean coveralls and join Doc and Uncle Ed who have almost finished the evening chores.

"Sorry we are late, boys," Pa says.

Doc and Uncle Ed give us a grin. Uncle Ed says, "You missed out on a great dinner."

I know they are teasing us. I'll bet not a word was said. I hope Ruthie doesn't live with the Carter sisters when she moves to Penn Yan to go to high school in the fall. They are not like us at all.

CHAPTER 14

▼

STRANGERS

I awaken to the sound of rain hitting my bedroom window. The Carter sisters will have a very wet ride to town. Perhaps they won't go. Oh, no, I want my home and family to be back to normal. It is raining hard. In fact it sounds like sleet hitting my window. They can't drive in sleet and we won't be able to go to Sunday school either. Well, that is something good. The bad part is that the mud will be back.

"Good morning Ma, good morning Ruthie," I say when I reach the kitchen. "Golly, it smells good in here."

"Those are the sweet rolls you smell," Ma says with a smile. "Ruth made them special with cinnamon, brown sugar, and walnuts. Hurry along with your chores so we may have a nice breakfast."

"Yes, Ma," I say as I climb into my coveralls and barn coat.

I do my usual chores with the goats, pigs and horses. Grooming Bess and Sally I save to last. I have just begun giving Bess a good brushing when I hear Pa calling me.

"Danny, come along now, breakfast is ready."

"Coming."

Ma and Ruthie have fixed an extra special breakfast of sweet rolls, scrambled eggs, fried potatoes, and sausage. While we are at breakfast, the adults discuss how our guests will spend their time with us waiting for the day to at least grow warmer. Rain is one thing, sleet and ice is another.

After breakfast, we gather in the front parlor. We bring in chairs from the dining room and sit in a large circle. Pa leads us in our Sunday service by reading from the Bible. He looks very uncomfortable doing this in front of our company. Ma leads us in the singing of a few hymns. She selects our most favorites, *Blessed Assurance, Amazing Grace,* and *Jesus Loves Me.* Our guests look displeased with Ma's hymn choice but they join in with the singing. They have very high voices.

Somehow I feel the Carter sisters look at us as uncivilized. I wonder how Ruthie feels about them.

After our service, I spend as much time as possible in the barns finishing my chores and doing a few extra jobs like sweeping out the granary. As it is Sunday I'm not supposed to be doing any unnecessary work, but I want to stay out of the house as long as possible. I have seen enough of the Carter sisters.

I spend a few minutes playing with Tabby and the other barn cats. Tabby is the only one who is tame enough to pick up. I give him a quick hug and pat on the head. I learned my lesson long ago about not trying to pet or pickup any of the other barn cats. They quickly become snarling, hissing, and clawing wild animals. The most fun is to give them something to play with. A dry corn stalk with its rustling leaves works very well. I run around on the barn floor dragging the corn stalk behind me. The cats have a wonderful time chasing and pouncing on the leaves.

Later, Mary, Carolyn, and I play quietly in the family parlor. Clara comes in for a visit, stretching mightily as she walks. We roll Carolyn's red ball for Clara to chase. Her tail is twitching as she crouches for the attack on the moving ball. She must think it is a running mouse. Sometimes she rolls head over heels to stop the rolling ball.

I'm watching the weather. The rain has mostly stopped. We eat a quiet late dinner. The Carter sisters pack their belongings. Pa asks me to harness their horse and hitch it to their buggy. I gave the horse a good grooming this morning and it looks much better than when I first saw it. I feel sorry for her though as she has been neglected. The horse is thin and its coat is dull and dry. I drive her to the side door.

"Are you sure you should make the long trip to Penn Yan?" Ma asks. "It is still quite cold."

"We have imposed on your hospitality long enough, Mrs. Lee. We really must be going. My sister and I always feel better when we are snug in our own home. Thank you for your kindness. We will discuss whether we would like to take your daughter in as a boarder for the next school year. She is a lovely young lady but is so unlike us. I will let you know of our decision soon."

I look at Ruthie's face. It is pink with embarrassment.

The stern old woman turns to me, "What did you do to my horse, young man?" she asks. "Abigail looks wonderful. Her coat is so glossy."

"I gave her my extra special grooming this morning," I say with a smile.

Pa gently says, "If I may say so, she needs more feed."

"Thank you, Mr. Lee. Perhaps our man hasn't been giving her the attention she should have. I will have a talk with him." With that remark, the two women turn to their buggy. Pa helps them inside and hands Miss Carter the reins which she immediately flicks on Abigail's thin looking back and they rattle on their way. We wave good-bye but they don't look back.

Ah, now we can return to normal.

Monday is another dark and dreary day. We children go to school. I'm glad to be at school as the men are using the manure that has been collected all winter to fertilize the grapevines. This work is done by loading manure onto an old wagon used for this job and drawing it to the vineyards. The men place a spade full of manure next to each vine. It is hard work that I am not asked to do.

Miss Spaulding and Ruthie quietly talk together during school recess. The look on my sister's face shows me she is very concerned about having to stay with the Carter sisters come September. I doubt she would be comfortable with them nor them with her. Perhaps they will tell our parents they don't wish to have her board with them. What will happen then? September is a long way off. A lot could occur between now and then, but I wish I could do something to help my sister.

Farm work is never finished. Doc and Uncle Ed are plowing for the corn and potato fields. Soon we will have two plows as Pa bought a Syracuse #1 plow at the Pulteney Hardware for nine dollars. Mr. Peck let him pay five dollars down. I would like to learn to plow but Pa tells me it is too hard for me to do. Perhaps next year I will be strong enough to help with the plowing.

Every night after supper the girls have been working on Ma's Easter dress. The dining table is cleared of everything and dark blue fabric, scissors, pin cushion, thread, and tissue paper pattern appear. Even little Carolyn helps as she is put in charge of collecting the scraps as they are cut. The dress parts are basted together and fitted to Ma. Mary helps with the basting but Ma and Ruthie do the actual finish sewing. Mary's stitches are not fine and even enough for finish work. She doesn't want to practice. I can't say that I blame her.

Some evenings I read aloud from the Charles Dickens book, *Oliver Twist*, Miss Spaulding lent to us. It sure is a sad story but one that ends well. How could anyone teach a boy to steal? Oliver received a little food and some emotional attachment but he was expected to steal from well-to-do men on the street. Much to his credit, Oliver knew stealing was wrong and resists as much as possible. We are most pleased by the ending of the story. The reader learns love and kindness is needed by all.

When the dress is almost finished, Ma says, "Mary, you and Carolyn may get down Grandma Lee's sewing basket from the top shelf of my wardrobe. Please choose three nice small buttons to close the neck of my dress." She shows them the picture that is on the envelope the dress pattern came in.

Ruthie is busy crocheting an edging to sew on the dress collar. The finishing touches for the dress are taking a long time.

"Come on Carolyn let's hurry. Looking at Great grandma Lee's buttons is going to be lots of fun," Mary exclaims. After what seems to be a long time, the girls return. "We can't decide among these, Ma," Mary says. Little Carolyn gravely nods her head.

"Put them on the table and we will have a vote," Ma says. Even Pa, Doc, and Uncle Ed gather around the table to help select the buttons. Three dark blue buttons with a sun burst engraved on them are picked as being just right.

One morning at breakfast Pa says, "I want you to come directly home from school today, Danny. Please drive Bess and the democrat wagon down to Sturdevant's to pick up the new plow. Bess will be harnessed so all you will need to do is make the hitch. The *Earl* is bringing

the new plow from the Pulteney Landing and should arrive at three-fif-
teen."

"Yes, Pa." Oh boy, something fun and useful to do. The men will be
able to finish the plowing work much sooner with two plows.

"Ma, may I ride with Danny tomorrow?" Mary asks. Hope is clearly
on her face.

"I don't see why not, Mary. You were a good help while Ruth and I
were busy in the vineyards. You deserve to do something new." I give
Mary a big grin as it will be fun to have her ride with me.

We rush home from school and I change into work clothes.

"Here is a blanket for your legs, children. Mary, do you have your
warm garments on?"

"Yes, ma'am."

"Say hello to Mr. and Mrs. Sturdevant for us," Ma calls as we drive
down the lane.

"We will," we shout. It is great to be trusted to do special things by
my Pa. It makes me feel grown up.

I drive Bess down the steep road to Sturdevant's Landing to pick up
the plow. Mary and I have a wonderful time looking for birds to iden-
tify. We see Canada Geese, a Red Tail Hawk, a pair of Cardinals and
some Chickadees. There are gulls flying over the lake. The sun is making bright sparkles on the blue water. We admire the view of the lake
and notice Mr. Sturdevant has his grape work done in the vineyards we
pass. He even has spread the manure.

I stop Bess at the big pier that is Sturdevant's Landing. There is no
one here. What will I do if the *Earl* doesn't arrive? I let Bess walk ahead
so she can drink from the lake.

"Where is the boat? How are we going to put the plow in the
wagon?" Mary asks. Concern is in her voice. "I know it must weigh a
lot."

"Don't worry, the men on the *Earl* will do it for us," I say. I am
checking the water level of the lake. Mr. Sturdevant has painted a water
level gauge on a leg of the pier.

Mary sees me studying the black marks and asks, "What is that for?"

"Mary, you have more questions than usual today," I say with a sigh. "That is a water level gauge Mr. Sturdevant made. It shows the water level to be high but not dangerously so. That means Aunt Liz and Uncle Jerome's house is not going to be flooded unless we have a lot more rain."

"How do you know that?"

"You see that wide black mark? That is flood stage and the level is several inches below that."

"Oh, I understand. That's good, isn't it? Where is the boat? I still don't see it."

"It will be along soon."

Uncle Philo and the two Stone brothers had launched the *Earl* last week. The steam yacht had spent the winter on the shore of Keuka Lake at Branchport.

"Look, the *Earl* is coming across the lake now." We had arrived at the boat landing in time to watch the steam yacht crossing the lake.

"Where, I can't see it," Mary cries.

"There," I point.

"Oh, yes, I see it now."

At first there is just a little speck with a dark cloud coming from it. There is little wind so the blue lake has few ripples. The speck quickly grows larger. Now I can see the white bow wave and know the *Earl* is at full steam. Soon the boat comes along the side of the pier and is tied up by the deckhand. I help with one of the lines and the young man gives me a smile and a little wave of thank you.

"Hello, Danny, hello, Mary. Good to see you," Mr. Howard Stone calls. He is the pilot for the *Earl* today.

We call, "Hello" in return and quickly climb board. There are two unfamiliar men setting in the stern of the boat. I wonder who they are. They are dressed in business suits, long dress coats, and have derby hats. One holds a leather case that appears stuffed with papers. They must have used a red plaid lap robe while crossing the lake. It is in a pile on the seat beside them.

"We have your Pa's plow, Danny. Back your wagon onto the pier so we don't have to carry it so far."

"Yes, sir, Mr. Stone."

I know the men are watching me as I carefully back Bess and the democrat wagon out on the pier. I must make this look easy. Mr. Stone, and his deckhand put the heavy plow on the wagon for us. They tie it to the front of the wagon box so it can't slide out while we are going up the steep hill.

Mr. Stone says, "Your Uncle Philo asked me to tell you the Baker and Amidon folks will meet you at the *Cricket's* landing in town for Easter Sunday services."

"Thank you, Mr. Stone. I will tell Pa."

One of the strange men walks up to Mr. Stone and asks, "Is there someplace where we can hire a carriage?" His voice is gruff and demanding.

"The owner of this boat landing, Mr. Harlan Sturdevant might rent you a rig. I believe he is in his barn this time of day," Mr. Stone says.

"Thank you," the unknown man says and walks toward the barn. His companion goes with him. He has the leather case under his arm. There are papers poking out of the top.

Mary and I climb onto our wagon seat and wave goodbye to Mr. Stone and his helper. I chirrup to Bess and we are on our way home. Looking back over my shoulder I see the *Earl* is already backing away from the pier. They have a schedule to keep.

"I wonder who those men are?" Mary says.

"They look like businessmen to me," I say.

"What are they doing here?" Mary asks.

"I don't know, Sis." I try to be patient.

We make our way up the steep hill. I let Bess set her own pace. We have plenty of time to get home before dark. We are quiet and just admire the sights. The sun is low in the sky and casting a different light on the lake. The east shore and hills have turned to gold.

Then I hear a distant noise behind us. Before Mary can speak, I say, "Hush. What is that sound?" The answer comes to me. It is the sound of galloping horses and rattling carriage. Who would be running horses up this hill? The strange men from the boat. That is who.

I direct Bess to the right side of the road as close to the ditch as I dare and draw her to a stop. I hope there is enough room for their carriage to get by.

I jump off the wagon and run ahead to hold Bess' bridle. Her ears are flat to her head and eyes wide open. Bess' huge feet are pounding the road. She is worried about what is behind her and wants to run away.

Mary is hanging onto the side of the seat. I can see she is afraid. "Mary, jump down and stand beside me."

"Those men are coming up from behind and will pass us, Mary. There is plenty of room for them," I say with my best big brother voice. Why did this have to happen at a narrow point in the road? There is nowhere to get off the road as there is a steep cliff on one side and a ditch and sharp drop off on the other.

"Why are they driving so fast?" Mary asks. "They are being mean to the horses." Her blue eyes are wide with concern.

"They sure are. Hang on here they come." The full noise of the galloping team has reached us. The horses and carriage with the two men in it come around the bend.

"Get that old farm wagon off the road, boy," one of the men shouts. "Make room for your betters."

I carefully lead Bess ahead so that the wagon's right wheels are off the road. The wagon is about to tip over and slide down the hill possibly taking Bess and us with it. I feel Bess doesn't want to stand on the side hill. She wants to be on the road where she has good footing. I pull Mary to stand ahead of Bess so the wagon won't hit her if it does begin to slide sideways.

The rapid moving horse's hooves kick up small stones from the road surface. Some hit Bess and I can feel her nervous energy. "Whoa, girl. It will be all right in a minute."

The team and carriage finally zoom by. One of the men is shaking his fist at us. What is the matter with him? Will the team be kept at that pace all the way up the hill? Mr. Sturdevant wouldn't like his horses to have to work that hard. Why do these men have to be so thoughtless? They gave us a very close call. Bess is very good and now stands quietly.

After they go by, I look at Mary. She has tears running down her face. "What is the matter?" I ask.

"I feel sorry for those poor horses."

"Yes, so do I. Perhaps the driver will slow them soon." I lead Bess ahead so that our wagon will be back on the road. After helping Mary onto the wagon seat I jump in and call, "Giddap Bess." We continue our slow way up the road and listen to the horses and carriage ahead of us. Finally we can't hear them anymore.

When we reach the top of the hill and turn right onto the Ridge Road, we can see the horses and carriage are waiting outside the Abraham Wagener mansion, Grandpa's old house. The horses are standing with their heads down and sides heaving. The men must be inside.

"I wonder if one of those men is Mr. Overhouser," I say. "I think the one who spoke to Mr. Stone looks like the man I saw in Penn Yan and when Uncle Ed and I were forced off the road last month."

"Please, let's get home before they decide to race down the Ridge Road," Mary pleads.

By the time we reach our equipment shed, the team and carriage are traveling north at full speed. The two lanterns are lit silhouetting the men. How is Mr. Sturdevant going to get his rig home?

Pa and Uncle Ed come out of the horse barn to unload the plow. "Who was that moving so fast on the road, children?" Pa asks.

I say, "Two men came across the lake on the *Earl*. I guess they hired a rig from Mr. Sturdevant. I think one of them is Mr. Overhouser. They had stopped at grandpa and grandma's house."

"They ran the team all the way up the bluff and now they are running them again," Mary says with tears in her eyes. "Won't they hurt the horses?"

"They could, Missy."

I look at Pa. He looks angry. "What could make them be in such a hurry as to endanger a team of horses? It sure looks like Mr. Overhouser is buying your grandpa's old place."

I hope the rest of his family isn't as thoughtless as he is. It seems like business is the only thing that matters to him. Mr. Overhouser is always in a hurry. All of the farmers on the bluff are friendly and helpful to each other. Why is he so unfriendly and rude?

Mary and I go into the house to change into work clothes as it is time to do chores.

Ma notices Mary has been crying and stops what she is doing to speak to her and give her comfort. Our Ma is good at giving us comfort when we need it.

I begin my usual chores and see our billy goat has returned and Mr. Goat is gone. Mr. Copson, the goat farmer from Branchport, must have come by. I say hello to Billy and give him a chance to recognize me. I think he remembers me. I'm glad to see him.

When I reach the house, Mary and Ruthie are nowhere to be seen. "Where are Mary and Ruthie, Ma?"

Ma says, "They are in the basement sorting through the potatoes to find the best ones to take to town with us tomorrow."

"What are these pies for?" I ask. I hope they are for our supper. "What kind are they?"

"Hands off, Danny. They are for Easter dinner tomorrow. They are apple."

I go down the cellar stairs to help with the sorting and to think about Easter dinner. Yum!

CHAPTER 15

▼

EASTER SUNDAY

Here we are, Pa, Doc, and me sitting in the parlor waiting for the girls. The democrat wagon has been cleaned and the extra seats placed inside. Our horses, Wild Andy and Toby have been specially well groomed and their harness polished to a bright shine. Bells are attached to their harness. Andy and Toby are hitched to the democrat wagon.

Uncle Ed has ridden Sally to the Marshall place to meet Miss Spaulding. They will ride together with the Marshall family. We will meet the *Cricket* at Sturdevant's Landing. Uncle Jerome and Aunt Liz will meet us at the landing too. The family will be attending Easter Sunday services in Penn Yan together. Easter is always a special event as we join relatives who live in Penn Yan.

We men are ready but are waiting for the girls to finish getting their hair fixed. First Carolyn and then Mary come into the room and carefully sit on the horse hair sofa. Their braids have pretty ribbon woven into them and bows tied on the ends. The girls don't want to wrinkle their dress or mess up their hair so they sit very still. It is funny to watch them but I don't laugh as being dressed up is very serious to them. I am dressed up too in my new suit with trousers in place of nickers. Ruthie and Ma are not to be seen.

"Ellen, are you about ready? We will miss the boat if we don't leave soon," Pa calls.

Ma and Ruthie come into the room and we men jump to our feet. Doc speaks first, "Missus, you look, ummm, you look, ummm."

"Lovely," finishes Pa. He gives Ma a little hug. Both Ma and Ruthie have their hair piled on top of their head like the town women do. I look at them in amazement. Ma looks beautiful in her new dark blue dress and Ruthie, looks like a young lady instead of my older sister. I guess she is a young lady.

I hear Pa whisper to Ma, "You look stunning in your new dress and with your hair that way!"

"Say something nice about Ruth too," Ma whispers to Pa. "Why, thank you, Charles. You look quite handsome yourself," Ma says in her normal voice.

"Your hairdo is very nice for this special occasion, Ruth," Pa says.

"Thank you, Pa," says a blushing Ruthie. "You look very grownup in your new suit, Danny. Now that you have trousers you will have to act like an adult."

"I'm going to try." I look at Mary, she is trying not to laugh. Our big sister likes to make snide remarks.

"Happy Easter to all," shouts Carolyn and Mary.

"Come on, everyone, lets get a move on," Pa says. "We have a boat to catch."

We meet Uncle Henry and his family on the Ridge Road and make our way down to the lake and Sturdevant's Landing. Uncle Ed and Miss Spaulding are already waiting at the pier with the Marshall family. We unharness our horses and turn them loose in Mr. Sturdevant's barnyard.

Shortly Uncle Jerome and Aunt Liz drive up in their buggy which is being pulled by good old Poky. Pa and I unharness him and put him with the other horses. Poky acts glad to see Andy and Toby as they are well acquainted. They touch noses and prance about the barnyard. They add a few snorts for good measure. The other horses watch them with puzzled eyes. Sally at first stands off to one side but then joins her stable mates. Andy and Toby are their usual wild selves and race about in the barnyard. The other horses avoid them.

Mr. Sturdevant's hired hand comes by to speak with Pa, Uncle Jerome, Uncle Henry and Mr. Marshall. "I'll take good care of your animals while you are away," he says.

Each man gives the hired hand ten cents to care for the animals.

We hear the toot of the whistle on the *Cricket* and soon see her come steaming toward us.

In a few minutes, the *Cricket* comes smoothly to a stop across the end of the dock. Uncle Philo is at the wheel and waves to us as we board the boat. Soon we are under way. Uncle Henry and Jay are speaking with Mr. Marshall. Uncle Philo's folks are already on the boat. Pa and I help find seats for the girls and climb the ladder to the pilot house.

"Good morning, Philo," Pa says. "Happy Easter, brother."

"Good morning, Uncle Philo," I say.

Uncle Philo has a big smile on his face and wishes us "Good morning and Happy Easter to you. You sure look good in that new suit, Danny."

"Thanks Uncle Philo."

Then he says, "Here, Danny, take the wheel for a minute. I want to show your Pa something in the engine compartment."

A feeling of shock, surprise, and doubt flow through my brain like lightning.

"But but, I can't steer this boat," I stammer. How can my hands become sweaty so fast?

"Sure you can. You have watched me many times," Uncle Philo says. "Just pull her out into the lake and head for the east shore."

"Go ahead, Son, you can steer the boat out into the lake while we are gone. We'll be back in a few minutes."

The two men climb down the ladder into the engine room. I'm left alone in the pilot house of a ninety-five foot long steamboat. I take the wheel in my two hands and look ahead. I can't see over the pilot wheel! I might have known I would be too short to steer the boat and look ahead at the same time. What can I do? Look out the side window of the pilothouse, of course, to see what steering is needed. A small turn to the starboard. I can do this. Turning the wheel clockwise pulls the boat further away from the shore.

Where are Pa and Uncle Philo? Why haven't they returned? I know our next stop will be directly across the east branch of the lake. I search the east shore for Richard's Landing. I can't see it yet but know about where it is. I spent part of a cold winter night there in February when I was lost in the dark. I shiver to think of the dark, cold night I spent on Keuka Lake ice.

The boat is picking up speed. Someone must have given the engines more steam. I wish my Pa or Uncle Philo were at the wheel. But it is wonderful to have all this power in my hands. I can do this. I know I can. I can steer this boat.

Now that we are away from Bluff Point, I turn the boat slightly north. I want to use Uncle Philo's spyglass to look for Richard's Landing but don't dare let go the wheel. I should be able to find the steamboat landing soon as there are lots of vineyards behind it. I hold the wheel with one hand and look ahead through the side window of the pilothouse. Ah, there is the landing.

"You did just right, Danny," Uncle Philo says from behind me. "I'll take her now."

I about jump out of my skin with the sound of his voice. I wonder how long he had been standing behind me. "Boy, was that exciting!" I exclaim. "Thanks for letting me take the wheel."

"You're welcome."

Pa gives me a pat on the back, "Good job." Pa is smiling his best smile. I know he is pleased with me.

I can't wait to tell the girls and Jay about my short adventure. Down to the cabin I run. After I have told my story, Mary and Carolyn look at me with admiration. Ruthie looks skeptical and Ma looks proud. Jay is pouting a little. I know he wishes he had been at the wheel of the *Cricket*. Boy, what a story I will have to tell my friends when I am at school on Monday.

We steam toward Penn Yan, stopping along the way to pickup passengers. The boat stops at Crosby Landing to collect the Amidon families and Great Grandma Baker. Many families are going to town to church on the Easter Sunday and to be with friends and relatives.

I watch Ruthie and Ma looking at the women and girls as they come into the cabin. They want to know how they are dressed. Ruthie is happy to show off her new hairdo. She doesn't have a new dress but she does have a fancy hairdo. Ma looks wonderful in her new dress and new hairdo.

When we reach the *Cricket's* mooring place along the Keuka Lake outlet, I look among the waiting carriages and buggies for Ma's brother, Mr. Alderman Baker, whom we call Uncle Aldy, and Mr. William Fenner, husband of Uncle Aldy's daughter, Ida. Uncle Aldy's wife is Carrie Monroe Baker. Cousin William is the accountant in Penn Yan that Billy Marshall works for. These families live on Brown Street in Penn Yan.

Aunt Carrie and Cousin Ida are already at the First Baptist Church on Main Street. We will be going to Uncle Aldy and Aunt Carrie's home for Easter dinner.

It will take several trips by cousin William and Uncle Aldy to get all the Lees and Amidons to the church. The Marshall family is going to the Methodist Church and Doc is going to his daughter's house. We will see them for the return trip on the *Cricket*.

The First Baptist Church in Penn Yan was built in 1871 so it has been in use for twenty-four years. It was the first brick building in town. We have many brick buildings now. The building is very fancy on the outside and has a tall steeple.

We arrive at the church just as services are beginning. The congregation and choir are singing *Christ the Lord is Risen Today*. The church is full, but people slide together on the pews and room is made for us.

I am sitting in the front row with Ma, Pa, and the girls. The pew
doesn't have any cushion. I sure hope the service doesn't last too long.

I'm fascinated by the beautiful organ and its shiny pipes. I am told
there are many more pipes that cannot be seen. They are hidden
behind a screen. The organ console is centered under the exposed
pipes. The choir members sit on straight back chairs on either side of
the organ player. In front of them is the pastor, Rev. A. K. Walrath.

All the wood in the church is dark stained oak. The windows are
beautiful multicolored stained glass. The pastor's sermon is long which
makes sitting on the hard pew difficult. I try to pay attention to what
the Rev. Walrath is saying: life is eternal if we follow God's rules. I'm

not sure I understand this but I will try to be a good and useful person. We sing several joyful hymns.

After Easter services have finished, the family begins its trek to Brown Street and Uncle Aldy and Aunt Carrie's home. Again, Uncle Aldy and Cousin William ferry the family in their carriages. We men begin walking to make the trip faster. By the time we reach Uncle Aldy's home, the women are putting the finishing touches on our family Easter dinner. Of course we have baked ham and mashed potatoes, three kinds of vegetables including scalloped corn, rolls and butter, and apple, cherry, and pumpkin pie. Wow! What a feast.

There are twenty-nine people eating dinner in the kitchen, dining room, and parlor. The younger children, including me, are in the kitchen. Someday I, too, will be with the adults. I guess wearing trousers doesn't make me an adult in the eyes of Aunt Carrie.

When dinner is over, Jay, Al, and I play outside. We are given warnings about not getting our good clothes dirty. Because of this, there isn't much we can do but walk around and look at houses and yards. It sure is strange to see so many buildings and people. I look up the hill to admire the huge Darius Ogden mansion. It is larger than the Abraham Wagener mansion on the tip of Bluff Point that I know so well.

"Hey boys, do you know the outlet is only a little way down this street?" Jay asks. "Let's walk over and take a look."

"Good idea," Al explains. "We can see what stuff has broken loose in the high water."

"Do think we should? I don't want to get my new suit muddy."

"You're still a momma's boy even in your suit with trousers," Jay says with a laugh.

"Well, I guess we can go there and just look. If you boys want to get muddy, go right ahead."

We carefully cross Lake Street avoiding all mud puddles. We walk between the buildings of the Sash and Blind factory that is silent today to get to the bank of the Keuka Lake outlet. Usually there is lots of noise and dust coming from this planning mill.

I don't know what there is about running water but it sure fascinates me. There is much mud here but I'm successful in avoiding it. The water is still flowing fast but no debris can be seen.

Jay says, "Aw, this is no fun. There is nothing unusual to look at here. Lets go back to the house and see if there is any left over pie we can eat."

"Good idea," I say. I'm glad to get back to the hard packed street with no mud on my clothes. We walk out on the Liberty Street bridge over the outlet to have one last look. Nothing but pea green water.

When we arrive at Uncle Aldy's house, we find there is only one slice of pumpkin pie left. We split it among us. We sit on the side porch and play with our yo-yos' until time to leave.

My family ride with Cousin William to the *Cricket's* mooring place. When all the Crosby, Bluff Point, and Branchport folks have arrived, we begin our steamboat ride home. We will be moving in the outlet channel in the semi light. By the time we reach the lake the sun has set and it is dark and cold. The lanterns on the boat have been lit and provide a golden glow. It is dark in the pilothouse so Uncle Philo can see the water ahead of the boat. We drop the Amidon folks and Great grandma Baker at Crosby Landing. We wave good-bye as they walk off the pier into the darkness. The last person I see is Cousin Bea waving to us.

Uncle Philo stops the *Cricket* at Sturdevant's Landing. As I walk down the gangplank, I think about Sally. Will she greet me or will she just tolerate me? In the darkness I feel someone next to me. It is Mary.

"What do you think, Mary, will Sally greet me like Bess does?"

"Yes, I think she will. In fact I know she will," Mary says confidently.

"Golly, I hope so." Mary gives my shoulder a comforting pat. Pa is lighting lanterns for us to use while harnessing the horses.

We are the first to reach the barnyard, lantern in hand. The horses are dozing in small groups. I quickly make out the gray bodies of Andy and Toby. My eyes search for Sally. I don't see her at first. I soon realize she is behind her stable mates.

The horses now know someone is at the barnyard. All heads rise with faces looking toward us. Ears are pricked. Eyes are wide open. I anxiously wait for Sally to see me. She does. Her ears point more forward, her lips move a little. I hear a soft nicker and she comes trotting to the fence where Mary and I are standing. She knows me and wants to be with me! What a wonderful feeling to know my little mare likes me.

Mary and I pat Sally's muzzle and rub the white streak on her forehead. "Good girl, Sally, I'm glad to see you too. You were right, Mary. Sally did greet me," I say happily.

Pa walks by us and says, "Help Uncle Jerome and saddle up, Danny. We have work to do at home. I see Sally has decided to be your friend."

"Yes, Pa. Isn't she wonderful?" Pa just smiles. He knew all along my mare would come to enjoy being with me. My kindness to her has paid off.

Uncle Ed is helping Uncle Jerome harness Poky. I only fasten the traces of his old buggy to Poky's harness. Uncle Jerome lights the two lanterns and helps Aunt Liz into the buggy. He slowly climbs onto the seat.

Uncle Ed says, "Do you want to lead the way or do you want to follow Miss Spaulding and me?"

"I'll follow along behind you. That way we can make sure you and Miss Spaulding aren't sitting too close." Uncle Jerome laughs his belly laugh. He reaches out of the buggy and gives Uncle Ed a pat on the back. Uncle Ed laughs too, but not very loud.

When we near the top of Bluff Point and the Ridge Road, the almost full moon is rising in the east. Its light is causing thousands of sparkling diamonds on the lake below. We will not need lanterns while working outside the barns and house when we reach home.

978-0-595-36084-0
0-595-36084-X

Printed in the United States
122285LV00009B/99/A